The Miracle

Books by Blaine M. Yorgason
and / or Brenton G. Yorgason

The Miracle
Chester, I Love You
Double Exposure
Seeker of the Gentle Heart
The Krystal Promise
A Town Called Charity, and Other Stories About Decisions
The Bishop's Horse Race
The Courage Covenant (Massacre at Salt Creek)
Windwalker (Movie Version)
The Windwalker
Others
Charlie's Monument
From First Date to Chosen Mate
Tall Timber (private printing)
From Two to One*
From This Day Forth*
Creating a Celestial Marriage (a text)*
Marriage and Family Stewardships (a text)*

*Coauthored with Wesley R. Burr and Terry R. Baker

the Miracle

Blaine M. Yorgason
Brenton G. Yorgason

BOOKCRAFT
Salt Lake City, Utah

Library of Congress Catalog Card Number: 83-72859
ISBN O-88494-510-3

2 3 4 5 6 7 8 9 10   89 88 87 86 85 84 83

Lithographed in the United States of America
PUBLISHERS PRESS
Salt Lake City, Utah

For all those who truly give

Acknowledgments

The authors express appreciation first to Larry Barkdull, a good friend who gave us the idea for this story; second, to the Crockett family for their selfless contribution; and finally, to Rita Palmieri Elkins and her mother, Mrs. Josephine Palmieri, who also helped and so became a part of the story.

Knowing

Consider this.

> Knowing is power,
>> you've heard that cliché.
> Yet it's also a burden,
>> with a price one must pay.

> Of course for some it seems easy
>> all precepts to live,
> But the rest of us struggle
>> obedience to give.

For instance,

> I'm a tale-teller,
>> a professional schemer,
> A believer in fantasy
>> and always a dreamer.

> Practicality in me
>> is hard-found as gold,
> Imagination's my focus,
>> for stats are so cold.

Yet,

> God's commandments are factual,
>> always vitally true,
> And my knowing of them
>> means my options are through.

> Pragmatism here now,
>> no tales and no dreams,
> For life is non-fiction,
>> with obedience themes.

Thus,

    I'm burdened by knowing
        I'm a dreamer who must do
    Or I'll lose self-respect
        and God's confidence too.

    But there's always a blessing
        when the hard way is taken.
    When knowing becomes doing
        we're lifted toward heaven.

                    —Blaine M. Yorgason

Contents

ONE

A Mountain Called Moose

Hey, Moose, wake up! She means *you!*"
Myron "Moose" Millett, startled from his reverie,
focused his mind just in time to hear the repeat announce-
ment.

"Myron Millett? Would Myron Millett please report to the
office."

Surprised, Moose stared at the speaker on the wall. He
had been daydreaming again, staring at Cassi Hancock and
imagining himself escorting her to the Christmas Ball. As far
as he knew, his and Cassi's names were the only nominations
for king and queen, and if he could only pull off a rare
victory . . .

Cassi was truly beautiful, and Moose was usually content
to simply stare at her. That day, though, it was more than
daydreaming. He could actually see the two of them, together,
and the vision in his mind was nothing short of heaven. She
was simply stunning with her long dark hair, her striking blue

eyes, her fair skin, her thin and graceful arms, her slender and perfectly formed hands, her devastatingly brilliant smile. In other words, to Moose as well as to everyone else he knew, Cassi Hancock was an absolutely gorgeous girl.

But what could they want him for in the office? Suddenly Moose remembered his sluff of the day before, and his heart sank. He'd not even thought of this, had not anticipated the penalty such a sluff would bring. His grades would of course be cut, but even worse, he'd not be allowed to run for king; he could not possibly win and stand beside Cassi, who was sure to win. Oh, no! Why hadn't he thought it through before sluffing?

"Hey, Moose!" someone behind him whispered, "what are you waiting for? An escort?"

There was a tittering of muffled laughter, and Moose could feel the blood start up his neck. He stole a glance at Cassi and saw that she too was smiling, and then a girl's voice came from behind him.

"Better hurry, Moose, or you'll miss Christmas, too."

The laughter was now loud and continuous, and Moose could feel his ears burning with embarrassment. Anxiously he pushed himself to his feet, and in doing so became entangled in the legs of the chair. He stumbled, lurched free, and as the chair crashed to the floor he saw Cassi again, laughing just like all the others.

Feeling worse than ever, Moose reached for his chair to right it, somehow kicked it instead, and sent the chair crashing into Ted Gomez's left leg.

"Watch it," Ted snarled in mock anger as he kicked the chair away. "That's the only leg I've got on that side, you clown."

"You know," somebody shouted as Ted shoved the chair back, "I think you spell Moose like this: K-L-U-T-Z!"

The laughter had now risen to a howl, and Moose realized that even the teacher, Mrs. Lomax, was out of control. Quickly, and feeling totally humiliated, he gathered up his books from the floor, looked bleakly at Ted Gomez, avoided Cassi's eyes, and then hurriedly made his way out of the door, doing his best to shut his mind and his emotions against the taunts and laughter echoing behind him.

Fighting back his tears of humiliation, Moose fled blindly down the hall, wishing that he could punch their lights out, wishing that he dared use his great strength to show them who he was, wishing that he hadn't promised his mother that he'd never fight, wishing with all his heart that Cassi had not seen him and had not laughed, wishing that he'd never been nominated as king, wishing that he'd sluffed school today as well.

And then, because he was not watching where he was going, Moose crashed headlong into a suddenly opened door. As he heard the laughter coming from that classroom he reeled past the door, steeling his mind against the physical pain that had now joined forces with his emotional agony, forcing himself against his will to continue toward the office.

"Dad," he anguished beneath his breath, "why did you do this to me? Why? Why do I have to be so big and so clumsy? Why can't I just be normal like the rest of the guys?"

After a hurried stop in the restroom to clean up, he finally pushed open the office door.

"I'm Moo—I mean, Myron Millett," he stammered. "Did somebody want to see me?"

"My gosh, you're big," the student secretary said as she looked up at him in awe. "What position do you play? On the football team, I mean."

"Uh—tackle, mostly," Moose answered, wondering why he always had to entertain questions about his size and about football. "That is, I did until I quit. Now, *who* wanted to see me?"

The girl's face clearly showed her surprise. "I'm sorry! I was only trying to be friendly."

"I—I'm sorry, too," Moose murmured, realizing that he had snapped at her. "I don't dare play, and I just get tired of people—"

"You? A quitter?" the girl questioned, half teasingly and mostly serious. "Well, I guess it takes all kinds, but you sure don't look like a—a . . . Anyway, Mr. Crockett, the counselor, wants to see you. He's in his office, down the hall."

Moose wheeled and exited, his frustration and humiliation still pounding within him. Why didn't people understand? Why was he always judged so wrongly? What was the matter that they couldn't see inside a person, couldn't look past his size or his shape to see his heart? The whole school was like that. That was why he had to find a way to get to know Cassi, to take advantage of the door of opportunity she had apparently opened for him.

He was a quitter, he thought, his mind now jumping to his conversation with the secretary. But not for the reason everyone believed. Only how could he explain his reasons without losing even more ground with his classmates? How could he tell the secretary that?

How could he explain that he had quit the team after falling on, and breaking, the leg of a teammate and the cartilage in the knee of an opponent? How could he describe what it did inside him to know that his size and strength and awkwardness had maimed two people, possible for life?

Just the recollection of those two events started him perspiring all over again. The snap of the bones and cartilage was still vivid in his memory; he could hear the screams, and the terrifying wail of the sirens, the same sound that had once signalled to him the death of his father. Yes, he had been a quitter, but there was no point in trying to explain to anyone why.

Outside the door labeled "Rod Crockett, Counselor," Moose paused and took a deep breath, wondering what was going to happen.

He thought again of his sluff, felt sick with the realization of what it had done to his chances with Cassi, and in that moment or so of hesitation worked back through it in his mind.

When he'd finally realized, only yesterday, that he was in

love and not just ill, he had piled his books back into his locker, shrugged into his coat, and sluffed the last two periods. He walked out without checking at the brightly decorated office, climbed into the one true pride of his life — the '55 T-Bird he had personally restored following his father's death — and drove through the heavy holiday traffic to the cemetery. There, in the cold winter air, he talked things over with his father.

"It's Cassi," he said, staring at the small headstone from which he had carefully brushed the snow. "I think I'm in love with her, Dad, and I don't know what to do. Cassi Hancock is her full name, and boy, is she something! I've never felt about a girl like I feel about her. Ever since yesterday when she stopped me in the hall and told me she had nominated me for king — it was just like all the feelings I have been carrying for her all these past months were suddenly set free and allowed to fly. I tell you, Dad, I really think I'm falling in love!"

Light snow had started falling again, and Moose lifted his face, letting the flakes dissolve against the warmth of his skin. He loved the peacefulness of falling snow, and he loved the Christmas season too. There was something special about it, something that suddenly seemed intensely romantic. Bright lights, special music, Santa Claus and gifts, fun, parties, boys and girls laughing together . . .

"The only snag, Dad, is that Cassi's already going with Ted Gomez. He's a creep, though. A real turkey. Every chance he gets, especially when Cassi is with him, he throws it back in my face that I quit the team. He claims I'm the reason we lost at State, and says I don't have any backbone.

"I honestly can't imagine what Cassi sees in him. And maybe she doesn't see anything. Maybe she's trying to break away from him. Maybe that's why she nominated me for king.

"Dan Hancock — he's Cassi's little brother and my best friend — he feels the same about Ted as I do, only he thinks my feelings for Cassi are hopeless. But I just can't throw out my feelings, Dad. They're real, and they're strong, too. I want her to be my girl friend. I really do. I've never wanted anything so badly in my whole life, except for—for y—you to be —be back with Mom and me."

Moose's tears started then, tears he'd vowed over and over through the past two years to dry up and put away forever. But somehow, no matter how he'd tried, thoughts of his father's death stirred them up every time. He missed his dad, oh, how he missed him! He missed his laughter, his teasing, his huge bulk lumbering around the house. He even missed his occasional outbursts of anger.

"But how do I go about it?" Moose continued, shifting his thoughts back to the present and glancing around the cemetery to regain control. "That's the problem, Dad. You know me. I'm so afraid of girls that I can't even talk to Cassi intelligently, let alone ask her out.

"Even when I go to her house to get Dan I get all tongue tangled when I see her. I'm sort of scared of her folks, too, because they live where they do and have all the things we don't have. It's funny that Dan doesn't make me nervous, but he doesn't. Maybe it's his big words and owl-eyes and toothpick-skinny body. The other kids tease him some, and maybe that's why he and I are friends.

"Anyway, Dad, what can I do? What would *you* do if you were me? There's got to be some way I can let Cassi know how I feel. There just has to be! Gosh, I wish I could talk to you, even for only a minute or so."

Through the door to Mr. Crockett's office Moose heard the telephone ring. The man inside answered and began talking, and Moose remained still, dreading the meeting, hating himself for not thinking ahead to the consequences of his sluff, and wondering what could be done about it. But there was nothing he could do now. It was too late. Besides, it was just like everything else in his life, confusing and somehow frozen into place so that, no matter what he did, it couldn't be helped.

Yesterday was an example, he reflected. After driving away from the cemetery, he made some resolves and then felt a whole lot better about things.

"Plan your work," his dad had always told him, "and then work your plan. Very rarely is anything good accomplished without preparation and perspiration."

This counsel was very much in Moose's mind as he nursed his father's restored T-Bird away from the cemetery and along the snowy state road. *All right,* he told himself, *let's see what I have. First, I think . . . no, I feel that I love Cassi Hancock. Or at least, I'm liking her more and more every day. Second, even though I'd like it otherwise, she is going with Ted Gomez, and will likely continue to do so, even though she probably sees through him.*

Moose sighed, and as the mellow voice of Bing Crosby drifted out of the radio singing of white Christmases, he stared at himself in the mirror.

Third, he then mused, *you are just like your father before you, a human mountain everyone calls Moose.*

Ruefully the young man looked down at his huge frame, a body which seemed almost compressed so that it would fit into the tiny cockpit of the small car. Six foot seven and probably still growing, blond hair and blue eyes, and two hundred eighty-six pounds of what everyone but his mother called fat, and which she called muscle and bulk.

Strangely, he suspected she was more right than the others, though that did little good when it came to his being teased. But he'd tried to lose it, he really had! Only diets didn't help at all, and the more he exercised the bigger he got, literally. And he was solid, though most folks wouldn't have believed that.

It's no wonder they call me Moose, he groaned inside again. *With my size, it's a miracle I'm not known as the Blimp. Doggone it, Dad, why did I have to get all my genes from you, and all my emotions from Mom? Why couldn't that have been reversed, so that I'd be little and tough instead of big and a cry-baby?*

Fourth, he sighed, as he approached the first traffic light in town, *my best and probably only friend is also Cassi's brother. Dan could be a plus, and even with his crazy lingo he could probably explain my true worth to his sister. All I have to do is get him to do it.*

Fifth, I inherited this car, and since everyone else is so nuts about it, I can assume that Cassi is impressed with it too. It may not be as new as Ted's Camaro, but it's at least as classy.

And sixth, he thought as he'd braked carefully to a stop at the red light, *I am just not in Cassi's league. So asking her out, especially while she is going with El Creepo Gomez, is out of the question.*

Summarizing that summarization, Moose concluded, *I count three plusses and three minuses, which come out a Mexican standoff no matter how I turn it. That means I have only to tip the scales in my favor, and Cassi will see the light and be mine. Too bad my weight alone can't do it. For once in my life it'd be worth something.*

Above him the red traffic light beamed in perfect harmony with the ornamental Christmas lights surrounding it, and Moose knew with a certainty that they were the same lights his father had helped string every year since before Moose was born.

"It doesn't make sense," he declared as he gunned his engine a little and waited for the light. "Why do such trivial things remain unchanged and such important things change so suddenly? I'll bet these lights are older than Dad even, but they're still here, while he—he's . . ."

And once again Moose's emotions broke loose.

Tiny snowflakes swirled against the windshield and melted instantly, and as the water beaded up, Moose swiped at his eyes, reached forward, and clicked on the wipers. Then, as he continued waiting for the light to change, thoughts of Christmas and his father faded and he concentrated again on the new focus of his life.

Moose, he asked himself as the wiper blades beat their even cadence *how are you going to do it? What are you going to do, now that Cassi has taken the first step, to win her away from Ted? What can you do to help her realize that in spite of your giant frame, you are worth being seen with?*

The light flashed green, and carefully Moose eased into gear and released the clutch, inching forward along the slippery road.

"Careful, Lady," he told his car quietly, just as he always did when he drove his T-Bird alone. "Dad thought a whole lot of you, and so do I. You're way too important to wipe yourself out in a silly storm like this."

Ahead of him a truck suddenly stalled, and Moose hit his brakes, skidded, and barely stopped in time to avoid a collision.

"What the —?" he muttered as he collected his wits. "You numbskull, you shouldn't . . ."

And with his heart hammering in reaction to his near miss, Moose turned the wheels of the classic T-Bird and pulled out around the truck, doing his best to smile and nod understandingly at the man inside. And he did understand, too. Some people were lousy drivers, other people were giant social retards. Everyone had problems, unless maybe it was Ted Gomez, who was rich, thin, good looking, athletic, and smart, and who would probably marry Cassi and become president of the United States if his luck held out. And all that in spite of spending his life tearing others down so as to make himself look good. For pete's sake, why did some people seem to have it all!

Well, he sighed again as he turned down Wise Street toward his home, *stop worrying about Ted and concentrate on your own problem. Ted's got Cassi, and somehow you've got to get her away. What can you do, big fella? What can you do?*

Now, as Moose stood outside Mr. Crockett's office recalling his thoughts of the day before, his big heart nearly broke. There was just no way he could ever let Cassi know how he felt. She was too popular, she was too sharp, and she was way too petite to be interested in a human mountain like him.

Moose thought again of her features — her flashing eyes, dark hair, and creamy skin, her five-foot-four-inch figure, her thin bare arms —

Bare arms? Wait a minute!

He considered again Cassi's arms, knew that they had indeed been bare, and suddenly an idea flared up in his mind. It was a crazy but exciting idea that would surely impress her and quite possibly enable him to justifiably ask her out on an honest-to-goodness date.

It was Christmas. He could give her a gift, a magnificent and terrifically expensive gift that would dazzle her like nothing else ever could.

Yes, sir, Moose thought as he leaned against the wall outside Mr. Crockett's door, that was exactly what he could do. He would give her an expensive wristwatch just prior to the dance. A gift like that would force her to take him seriously, would obligate her to accept another date, and then she would become aware of the person he really was — instead of what he appeared to be.

Moose thought through that, felt the mounting excitement of the idea, and was just beginning to work out the logistics of getting a job and of paying for such a gift, when he remembered again his sluff.

As the painful facts of life jarred his mind, he knew his plan would never work. He would be forced to resign, would not be with Cassi at the dance, would never have a few moments alone with her when she was thinking of him, would not even stand by her side there.

The sound of silence in Mr. Crockett's office pulled Moose back to painful reality, and he stared again at the closed door, his heart beating faster. The counselor was off the telephone. That meant it was time to face the music.

Taking a deep breath to steady his wildly gyrating nerves, Moose raised his huge clenched fist and, squaring his shoulders, finally knocked.

"Myron," Mr. Crockett said, arising and extending his hand as the boy entered. "How are things going?"

"Okay, I guess."

"Good. Sit down, and I'll be with you in a minute."

Moose slumped into the chair, subconsciously doing his best to lower his frame to eye level with Mr. Crockett. As the counselor finished filling out a paper, Moose looked around. The office was small, little more than a cubicle, but it was jammed with things of interest. There were some posters that pointed out the evils of smoking, drinking, and drugs; there were pictures of the Crockett family; there was an autographed portrait of Donny and Marie; there was a painting of a tiny earth surrounded by black space, and off to the side a large finger pointing at the earth over the caption, 'Your time has come, my son.' There were also a couple of plants; on the file cabinet was a bottle with a miniature human skull on top; and a stuffed monkey hung crazily down the side of the cabinet.

Moose was looking at that monkey and wondering how it stayed put when Mr. Crockett suddenly spoke.

"How's your mother, Myron?"

"Fine, sir. At least, she was this morning when I left home."

Mr. Crockett smiled. "Tell her hello for me, will you?"

Moose nodded. *Here it comes,* he thought, his heart still bitter with the thoughts and experiences of the past few moments. *Here comes the sluff, the trial without jury, the order of execution, and no more king, no more hopes of Cassi.*

"Are you ready for Christmas, Myron?"

Surprised by the question, Moose dumbly shook his head.

"Neither am I," Mr. Crockett responded. "But I'm glad it's here. I think Christmas is my favorite time of year. The music of Christmas has a uniquely satisfying spirit, and I never tire of listening to it. The decorations, all of them, are fun, and somehow they help create a spirit of happiness that is almost impossible to describe. Do you know what I mean?"

Still silent, and wondering what all this had to do with his sluff, Moose nodded.

"And most of all," the counselor concluded, "I love what Christmas seems to do to people. They smile more, they usually act happy, and for once in the year they spend at least a portion of their time being considerate of others.

"I don't mean that to sound negative, Myron, but I'm a realist, as you probably remember. Besides, I'm about the same as most other folks. Life's complicated and busy, and it's easy to get all wrapped up in my own problems, leaving too little time to think of or be concerned about the people around me. I suppose that's why I really like Christmas. It forces me to become a little better person than I normally am."

For a moment Mr. Crockett studied the papers on his desk. Then he turned and looked Moose straight in the eye. "Well, Myron," he said evenly, "speaking of being a better person, do you want to tell me about yesterday?"

A thousand excuses raced through Moose's mind, but finally he decided it would save time if he just told the truth. "I went to the cemetery," he answered simply. "I was talking to my dad."

For a long moment Mr. Crockett looked at Moose. Then, leaning back in his squeaky chair, he clasped his hands behind his head and smiled.

"Do you do that a lot?" he asked.

"Not really. Not enough, I guess."

Again there was a quiet pause. Moose studied the floor while Mr. Crockett studied him. Finally the counselor spoke. "Well, we have a policy here that if kids are with their parents it isn't sluffing. Seems to me you have a pretty cut-and-dried excused absence."

Startled, Moose looked up. Mr. Crockett winked, and immediately Moose knew he did have another friend, one he'd never even thought about.

Actually he'd known Mr. Crockett a long time, had even been in his ward when he was serving as bishop, and had been his home teaching companion. But still, until now he'd not thought of that, had not remembered the man's kind and gentle ways.

Maybe, Moose thought, his big heart beating wildly, maybe now, after his dance plans had been reprieved, Mr. Crockett could help him with his plan to date Cassi. Maybe he could tell him of his idea and the counselor could help him refine it, could perhaps suggest some things Moose hadn't thought of.

Sure he could! Mr. Crockett knew Cassi, and would surely have some ideas!

"Uh—bishop, uh—I mean, Mr. Crockett, I have a real problem."

"Yes," the counselor replied. "I heard about it."

Moose looked at him in surprise. "You did? But—but how?"

"Word of that sort of thing travels fast, Myron. I found out about it yesterday, probably when you did. I don't blame you at all for skipping school. If I had been you I'd have probably . . . well, you look like you're handling it well."

Moose was thoroughly confused. How could Mr. Crockett have heard about his feelings when he hadn't even told Dan about them, let alone anyone else?

"What are you going to do about it, Myron?"

"Well, I had an idea today, but to pull it off I need lots of luck and a job, a *good* job. Can you give me any recommendations?"

"A job?" Mr. Crockett echoed, his voice showing his own surprise. "What on earth does a job have to do with it?"

"It's the money, sir. Don't you see? With enough money I can buy something really spectacular for her, and then she'll—"

"Myron, are you talking about the same thing I am?"

"I—I guess. You mean Cassi?"

"Yes, her and Ted Gomez and the others."

"Ted?" Moose questioned. "The others? But I don't—"

"Myron, I'm speaking of your nomination as king of the Christmas Ball. I'm speaking of Cassi's nomination of you, and now of Ted's nomination as well."

The counselor's voice reflected his surprise at Moose's blank expression. "You don't know anything at all about what I'm talking about, do you?"

Slowly Moose shook his head, his mind whirling with the news. Ted's nomination! Oh, no, that couldn't be! Not when Moose had set such hopes on becoming king!

Mr. Crockett, sensing the youth's confusion and wanting to understand it, wisely changed the course of the conversation. "Myron, if it isn't too personal, I would very much like to know what were you discussing with your father?"

Moose shook his head. "It isn't too personal, I guess. Not to keep from you. I was talking to him about Cassi. I was trying to think of a way to get her mind off Gomez—and on —on me."

"Do you like her?"

"Yes, sir. A lot."

"Have you dated her?"

"Oh, no! I want to, though. I'd give almost anything if I had the nerve to do it. And Dan—that's her brother—Do you know Dan?"

"Yes, I know him. The young man with the tautological tongue."

"Tauter what? Well, whatever! Anyway, Dan tells me I'd be . . . well, I'd be Cassi's *salvation* if I could get her to stop dating Gomez.

"Mr. Crockett," Moose continued, fully into what he was saying, "that's why I figured I ought to do something for her, like get her an expensive gift or something, just to encourage her feelings. I mean, you should have seen her when she took my arm and told me she had nominated me and she hoped I would win."

"That's interesting," Mr. Crockett replied slowly. "Very interesting. And you say you're looking for a job?"

Moose nodded, sensing at last that he was being understood. "You see, I can't afford a gift like I want to give her, but if I had a job, a good job, then I could swing it. Am I—am I making sense?"

"Oh, yes." The counselor smiled. "You're making sense. I just don't know if . . ."

Mr. Crockett paused and stared for a moment at his interlocked fingers. "Let me check around, Myron. Jobs are scarce right now, but I'll look. Meanwhile, whatever it is you're thinking of doing, think it through carefully. In addition, I'd suggest you get to know Cassi better, and she you, before you do something of such magnitude."

"That's what I'm trying to do, sir."

"I understand," Mr. Crockett replied, smiling. "As to this other issue of nominations, I would like to do some further checking. Give me a day or two to work on it, and I'll get back to you as quickly as I can."

Still not understanding exactly what Mr. Crockett was talking about, Moose stood. "Thank you," he said as they shook hands. "Thank you for the excused absence, and thank you also for listening. Any help you can give me with Cassi would be great."

"You bet, son. But don't you get your hopes up. About the job, I mean."

"I won't, but thanks anyway."

"Moose," Dan exclaimed later that afternoon as he rode with his friend through the downtown traffic, "I've stated this before and I'm reiterating it once again. This is far and away the most specious automobile in this locality."

"Well, I'm not sure what you just said," Moose answered, grinning, "but this baby *is* a fine car."

"I'm serious," Dan replied quickly. "This is an indubitably fine vehicle, of flawless style and consummately sleek lines. It should be worth a great deal of money, as my father was saying just the other day. I told him, though, that because of it's origin your car was worth even more to you than it otherwise might be."

"You're right there, little buddy. To hear my mom tell it, Dad's purchase of this car nearly brought about their divorce. Mom called it his toy, and they struggled for years to pay for it. I guess it's about all I really have left that links me with my dad. Mom says he fussed over it almost as much as he did over her — and I guess I do the same."

"Well, I understand those links and sincerely appreciate them," Dan said. "And you have every reason to feel proud of your work on it. You've done an excellent job of restoration. The facts of the matter are completely indisputable. Why, for proof, just observe how people stop and gape with slacked jaw as you motor past. This car is the envy of the entire student body, not to mention the community."

"Dan," Moose said as he looked at his friend, "if I ever get used to the way you sling words around, it'll be a miracle."

Dan smiled briefly, and then was instantly serious. "Yes, I understand your problem with my syntax, Moose, and I am empathic to it. Even my father considers my elocution somewhat pedantic, and his own vocabulary is far more obstreperous. But Moose, I am lonely and, save for you, without friends. Since I am neither athletic nor handsome, I study and enhance my vocabulary in the hope that I might in that small way stand tall among my peers."

"Well, it works, doesn't it?"

Dan sighed. "Unfortunately, yes. To my detriment. And now it is a habit which I seem unable to break."

"I don't think you should stop," Moose encouraged. "Mom says habits like that become more valuable as we get older. Kids don't appreciate them, but I'll bet adults will."

"I hope so, my friend. I wish I could do *something* as well as you have done in bringing to pass the restoration of this car."

"Thanks, Dan. It's been a lot of work. But you know, I

don't think very much of myself, either. I mean, look at me. I truly wish I were as classy as this car. Maybe if I were your size, I could—"

" 'Tis a twist, my friend, a royal twist. Why do you suppose it is that one always seems to desire what one lacks? Personally I lack size and strength, and therefore intensely desire those very qualities you carry in such abundance. In fact, I am certain that I desire them as much as you desire a romantic relationship with my sister Cassi, which you also lack."

"Yeh, that's a good point, Dan. And in fact, that brings me to the issue at hand. I'd like you to accompany me *post haste* to a certain local jewelry emporium. See, now *I'm* talking like you."

Dan, ignoring the final remark, gasped in surprise. "Jewelry emporium? Moose, no! Even if Cassi *did* accept a ring, which she most certainly wouldn't, my father would dismember your carcass piecemeal!"

Moose grinned even more widely. "Yeh, I'll bet a ring would shake a few people up. But stop worrying, Dan. Much as I'd like to, I'm not buying her a ring."

"Oh," the boy gasped, "thank heaven for benign blessings."

"Well, anything's better than malignant ones," Moose retorted. "Anyway, Dan, it isn't a ring. I'm thinking of giving Cassi a nice watch, an expensive one."

"But Moose, setting aside the problem of your lack of interpersonal rapport with my sister, how can you afford such a gift?"

"I can't right now, but I'm working on getting a job. If I do, there should be no problem."

"You're serious, aren't you?"

"Absolutely! I've got to find a way to encourage your sister to like me, and this method seems to fit the bill."

"Well, frankly, I *would* delight in seeing my sister's relationship with Theodore Gomez terminated. But Moose, I sincerely question whether she is indeed your type, and whether she would ever think of you as more than a passing giant."

"Dan, *I* decide who is my type, not you. Cassi's a sweet and unusual girl, from a very special family, and I'd like to do something that would show how I feel toward her. I'm going to get her a watch, and one way or another I'll find a way to pay for it."

Dan sat back and stared ahead. "Moose," he finally declared, letting his breath out as he spoke, "it seems to me that you would be making a great mistake, giving Cassi — or any girl, for that matter — a gift like that."

"I don't think so, Dan. She's used to things of quality, so it wouldn't overwhelm her that way. But a gift like that *would* tell her not only that I cared, but how much I cared as well."

"Oh, my large but foolish friend, you don't know her like I do. She wouldn't appreciate in the least such a gift as you are suggesting. Cassi's having a significant conundrum right now with selfishness, and in my opinion she's an enigma, beautiful on the outside and yet about as haughty and arrogant on the inside as —"

"Dan, don't you dare talk about Cassi like that."

"Hey, Moose, she *is* my sister, and I know. She *laughs* at you!"

Moose, momentarily silent, also stared ahead. "I know she laughs sometimes when I'm being teased," he finally said. "I don't blame her, either. I'm not an athletic hero like Ted Gomez, I'm terribly big, and besides, I'm a real klutz, and you know it."

"And even knowing how she feels, you *still* want to buy her a watch?"

"Dan, it's the only solution I can think of. If a couple more guys are nominated, it might split the votes enough to give me the crown. If so, then I'll just give my gift to her after the ceremony. That way she'll know of my appreciation for being nominated, and she'll also know how I really feel about her."

Dan looked carefully at his stubbornly insistent friend. "Moose," he asked slowly, "don't you know?"

"Know what?"

"Uh—well—about the nomination?"

"I know it was an honor to be nominated by Cassi. Just knowing she thinks that much of me is pretty great. Don't you think so?"

Again Dan studied his older and larger friend, wondering what he should say, how much he should spell out. But what good would it do? he decided. Moose was hopelessly under his sister's spell, and nothing he could think of, short of absolute murder, would bring him out of it.

"Uh—come on," he finally said, deciding to say nothing further until he had proof that would be totally convincing even to his friend. "You were going to take me window shopping for a watch. Let's go do it."

At the next corner, which was Main, Moose turned right and pulled to the curb in front of Reid's Jewelry. He and Dan climbed out, splashed through the melting slush to the window, stopped, and stood staring at the display inside.

"Well, what do you know!" Moose muttered in surprise. "There's the one I want."

"Which one?" Dan asked, a knot forming in the pit of his stomach.

"That one, on top of the pedestal. I saw a picture of it today in a newspaper ad."

Dan gasped. "Merciful heavens, Moose, have you perchance observed the price on that resplendent trinket?"

Moose nodded, a satisfied smile working across his face.

"Then have you run a cost analysis, my friend? I mean, have you considered the implications of such an expense upon your funds, which I *know* are rather limited?"

Again Moose nodded. "I know it's a lot, Dan. But remember, it's for Cassi. If this watch does what I'm hoping it will do, it'll be more than worth it."

Dan rolled his eyes in disgust, turned to some imaginary ally standing next to him who had almost equal mental powers, and began a lengthy discourse to that nonexistent person regarding the sad fact that brains did not grow in proportion to the bodies that housed them.

For a long moment Moose stood still in the sleeting snow, his big hands in his pockets, ignoring his smaller friend and trying to decide what to do. A woman walking past gave Dan and then Moose a funny look, and Moose, embarrassed, grabbed his friend's arm.

"Come on, little buddy. We're going in."

"No," Dan groaned. "I propose that we only observe today. I propose further that the purchase be made another time, after you have fully examined all the data—"

"Dan, knock it off, will you? Why are you acting so strange?"

"Moose, the size of the mistake you are about to make as you seek to impress my nonimpressionable sister is staggering in scope as well as in implication, and I refuse to be party to—"

"That does it," Moose growled, encouraging Dan through the door in a most definitive fashion. "We've got some shopping to do for one very elegant young lady."

Very much together, the two of them entered the store.

"May I help you?" the jeweler asked, peering up through his much-magnified glasses.

"I—I hope so," Moose replied, only slightly loosening his grip on Dan's neck. "We—I mean, *I* want to put a watch on layaway."

"Fair 'nuff. Which one?"

"Uh—the gold one in the window, on top of that little pedestal."

"Oh, yes," the man exclaimed, smiling. "A wonderful choice. Very expensive, of course, but it's a fine timepiece. Uh —is it for your wife?"

Dan snickered and Moose was totally embarrassed. "Well,

uh—no," he blurted. "I'm not married—uh—yet, I mean. I mean, I'm still in high school. It's—it's for a—a girl I know."

"Ahhhhh," the man smiled, winking. "I understand. And that watch is a *fine* bauble with which to impress a young lady. Something as expensive as that will sweep her right off her feet. As if you aren't big enough to do it anyway. Ha, ha."

Moose grinned faintly, Dan looked suddenly ill, and the jeweler, made nervous by the young man's awesome size and his friend's obvious disgust, spoke again.

"Uh—we normally take a ten percent deposit for lay-aways."

"Ten percent!" Moose gasped. "But that's—that's . . . Uh —I don't have that much. With me, I mean. Couldn't you do it for—for five dollars?"

"Five *dollars*?" the jeweler questioned incredulously.

"Yes, sir, it's all I have. With me, I mean. I don't want you to sell it to anybody else, and by Christmas I'll have enough to pay it off."

"Well . . ." The man hesitated. "I don't know you, and—"

"Sir," Dan said, suddenly interrupting, "permit me to introduce myself. I am Daniel G. Hancock, and I wish to verify the integrity and probity of this good man. Normally I would remain silent concerning this, for I do not approve of the purchase he intends, not at all. Nevertheless, I must stand up and be counted when the life and standards of my friend become the issue.

"You see," Dan continued, putting his hands firmly on the counter, "he is complaisant by nature, filled with a rare benevolence, has an ardor toward the needs of others, and is scrupulously without guile, maintaining unbounded integrity and completely candid veraciousness. His sincere comportment, in fact, has consummately astounded more than one of our fellow citizens, and furthermore, I would state with total and emphatic audacity—"

"Whoa!" Moose objected, grabbing his friend before the

jeweler could get his mouth open any wider and perchance end up with lockjaw. "Sorry, sir. He gets a bit windy."

"Windy! That kid's a veritable hurricane. What does he eat for breakfast? Dictionaries?"

"No," Dan replied angrily as he twisted away from Moose, "alphabet soup and thesauruses! And there, Moose, is a prime example of how much adults appreciate my study and talent!"

"Please, sir," Moose pleaded, doing his best to get on with the business at hand. "It's for a very special girl, and I really will make good on buying it."

For a long moment the man looked up into the gentle blue eyes of the lad who loomed above him, then he broke into a grin.

"Young love always gets to me," he said slyly. "I remember a couple of early romances of my own. Besides, how can I say no to someone as big as you are? Especially when you have a friend who can make chin music like that."

Embarrassed and altogether uncomfortable, Moose shuffled his feet and extracted his wallet from his hip pocket.

"Here's the five dollars," he said quickly. "I'll be back before the twenty-third to get the watch. And thanks, sir. Thanks a lot!"

"You're welcome. And, son," the jeweler continued, winking up at Moose, "may I suggest that you keep that jaw-flapping friend of yours on a leash? One of these days he'll pay someone a nice polite compliment and get arrested for vulgarity and defamation of character."

Dan growled and lunged forward, but with a quickness that belied his size Moose reached out and once again grabbed his friend by the back of the neck.

"Come on, little buddy," he mumbled. "Let's get out of here."

"Wait a minute!" the jeweler called as Moose started to herd Dan back through the door. "I don't even know your name. How can I put this watch on layaway without your name and address?"

"Uh—I'm sorry. I forgot. It's Moose—uh, I mean Myron. Myron Millett. And we live on Wise Street, 764 Wise."

"Moose, huh?" the jeweler grinned as he filled out the form. "It fits, you know. It really fits!"

"I know," Moose replied dejectedly as he turned to leave. "Oh, *how* I know!"

Moose sat in Mr. Crockett's office waiting for the counselor to appear. He stared at the poster showing the two lungs, one black from tobacco and cancer and the other pink and healthy, and he decided one looked about as gross as the other. "I'm certainly glad," he muttered to himself, "that I'm not going to be a doctor."

His eyes shifted to the poster with the big hand pointed at the tiny earth, and for the hundredth time since the day before, he found himself wondering what was going on. Something had happened that involved him and Cassi and Ted, but he'd not even spoken to Ted since the day of the nominations and he couldn't imagine what it could be.

Dan had heard of it as well, or at least what he'd said the night before led Moose to think so. But even he, with his overcharged tongue, couldn't be induced to say more. So what could it be? What connection, other than coincidence, did the nominations have?

Suddenly the door opened and Mr. Crockett entered. Moose quickly stood, and again they shook hands.

"You know, Myron," Mr. Crockett said, looking up at the young student, "I think you get taller every day. I'm six foot four, and you make me feel short. How much have you grown since I was your bishop?"

Moose shrugged. "Two or three feet, I guess. Mom says I've grown that much."

"At least," Mr. Crockett agreed, smiling. "Is your mother getting along all right—I mean, without your father?"

"Yeh, mostly. She says she wishes you were still our bishop."

Mr. Crockett laughed. "Well, some days so do I. We had a great time in that old ward. Your mother and father were two of my best supporters. I remember standing beside your father when he confirmed you a member of the Church. He was a big man, but I think you're bigger."

There was a moment's silence. Mr. Crockett placed his fingers together and drummed them against each other, and at last he looked at Moose and spoke.

"You know," he said, "you have the same color of eyes as my wife, Kathy."

"I do?" Moose asked in surprise.

"Yes. And I'd never thought of it before, but I suppose the old fellow's eyes *could* be the same blue as yours and hers. He's probably a big man, too."

Thoroughly confused, Moose stared at the counselor. What on earth was he talking about? Eyes? His wife, Kathy? Old fellow? Big?

"Myron," Mr. Crockett continued unexpectedly, "I called a few places about jobs. Most had nothing, but I did have a positive response from Maxwell's Department Store, where my wife works. You seem to have applied there some time ago for a stockboy position?"

"Uh—yes, sir, I did."

"Good. That shows initiative, and besides, it put you on their list. Surprisingly, they do have an opening, but my wife suggested that I discuss it with you. It—uh—it isn't exactly what you had in mind."

"Well, it doesn't really matter what the job is," Moose declared, feeling a sudden surge of elation. "I'll clean the floors or stock the shelves or do anything they ask. I just need the job."

Mr. Crockett laughed. "Well, let me tell you about it. I think you'll be surprised, and I hope you'll be intrigued. Personally, I think you could do it. Like I said, you have the eyes and the size, and I think you could do it well."

Calmly, Mr. Crockett explained the job opportunity to Moose.

"Santa Claus!" Moose blurted in response a moment or so later. "They want *me* to be their *Santa Claus*?"

"Myron, you're perfect for the job," Mr. Crockett enthused, smiling sincerely. "Besides — and this is the best part of the deal — they're willing to pay you union wages. They've used union men in the past, but the woman you interviewed with, my wife's assistant, was impressed with you. Kathy says she'd really like you to take a shot at it. What do you say?"

"But — but why me? Because I'm big and fat, right?"

Rod Crockett leaned back in his swivel chair, which as usual squeaked complainingly, and once again he smiled disarmingly.

"Myron, to be perfectly frank, I don't think your weight has much to do with their decision. Thin people can be made to look heavy. However, it is a very exhausting job. In the past they've gone through about three Santas in a season. You're big, as you say. You also look strong to Kathy, and she's counting on that.

"Besides — and this is far more important — Kathy's assistant liked your smile. She said you seemed especially gentle, and that was very important to her. Only gentle people, she told my wife a little while ago, ought to ever represent Santa Claus. Now, will you do it?"

"Santa Claus," Moose repeated almost to himself. "Me? Santa Claus? Well, I guess it's better than being nothing, which is what I am now. Santa Claus Millett. It doesn't sound too bad. Yeh, Mr. Crockett, I'm on."

Then he added, "Uh — you won't tell anyone else about this, will you?"

"No, not if you don't want me to. But why?"

Moose stared at the floor. "I — I guess I'd feel like that monkey hanging there on your cabinet, on display to be laughed at. Mr. Crockett, I'm already laughed at enough, and I'm not sure how much more I can take."

Mr. Crockett nodded understandingly.

Smiling then, Moose stood up. "If you promise to keep it confidential, I guess I'll try it."

"I hoped you would." Mr. Crockett rose also. "But Myron, there's something else, something perhaps even more important than the job. You mentioned your feelings for Cassi Hancock. Perhaps, if you have another few minutes, I could share something with you."

The two sat, and Mr. Crockett began to describe what was to be one of the most difficult things Moose had ever heard in his life.

"You've been the brunt of a very unfortunate manipulation," the counselor said. "I've visited with those involved, and because you've been used, I think you should know about it."

Moose nodded, and quietly but very earnestly Mr. Crockett began his narration.

Driving slowly forward through the early evening Christmas traffic, Moose again thought through Mr. Crockett's revelation, examining in detail each of the events that were now troubling him so greatly. Why had they done it? he anguished. Why did people do such nice things for such wrong and rotten reasons?

Cassi had nominated him for king of the Christmas Ball, Ted Gomez had seconded the nomination—and it had all been a set-up. The whole intent had been to have Ted nominated the following day, so that he would be running against Moose. That way, with Moose as competition, Ted would be sure to win—thus insuring a storybook finish with Ted and Cassi sharing the honors, and the evening, together.

Why? Moose asked himself. Why did something that had seemed so natural and good have to be so bad? Of course, Moose was certain that Cassi had known nothing of it. Why, the way she had told him of her nomination, the way she had slipped her arm into his, and the way she had gazed so earnestly up into his eyes, all proved her innocence. She couldn't have been simply acting. Nor would she have ever given him false hopes, false expectations.

No, such an idea had to be Ted's. But why? Why?

The more Moose considered the thing, the more upset he became. In fact, he was more angry than he could ever remember being—incensed at Ted Gomez. And his anger wasn't just because of his personal humiliation, either. It was because of what that—that *idiot* was doing to Cassi. It wasn't fair to her. She shouldn't have to be exposed to such stupid and degrading ideas and actions.

"Yaaagh," he snarled through gritted teeth. "Gomez, if you were here right now, there wouldn't be enough left of your miserable hide to cover a stuffed peanut!"

Now, as he drove through the night, Moose found growing within him an even deeper resolve to follow through with his plan, to do all in his power to relieve Cassi from her bondage to Ted Gomez. She was worth so much more than Gomez was giving her! And *he*, Myron Millett, was going to see that she got it.

"Dad," he said aloud, staring blankly at the road in front of him, "I hope you're listening, because now I *really* need your help! Christmas is the key, because it opens the door. I can give Cassi my gift legitimately and get the ball rolling. Whatever it takes, I'll do it. And that, Dad, is a promise!"

TWO

Another Perspective

At Maxwell's Department Store Moose was interviewed by Mrs. Crockett concerning his new job. Moose had never known Mrs. Crockett well, but he quickly found that she was sweet and kind and extremely talkative. She was also bubbly, and he couldn't help but become infected with her contagious enthusiasm.

"You'll *love* it," she said over and over after she had hired him, and before long Moose began to forget how silly being Santa Claus had seemed. In fact, before the interview was over he was actually looking forward to his first shift.

"Now come with me," Mrs. Crockett ordered as she led him to the rear of the store. "We've got to get you fitted and get a seamstress busy stretching that suit out. You know you were hired because of what my husband said about you, don't you? Nadine, my assistant, thought she'd never hear the end of all your wonderful qualities.

"Here's where you'll come each day to change, and of course you'll get an employee's discount on certain of our merchandise. Just see me when we have a little time and I'll give you the details, but don't expect miracles. Just today I've had to turn down sixteen requests from employees, and I've hardly had time to conduct my three other interviews, get all my shopping done for the weekend, get my office cleaned, and so on. And all that was done *after* I had walked three miles with my neighbor this morning, baked a batch of bread, mopped the floors, and made a wire-reinforced hat for my son's school party—which I have to go to in an hour.

"Oh, I forgot to tell you about your salary. I can't remember what you're starting at, so I'll have to find out, and one of these days when there's a little more time just ask me and I'll tell you. . . ."

Moose, grinning in spite of himself as Mrs. Crockett rattled on, was not even offended as the seamstress stared at him, gasped, and climbed on a chair to measure his neck and shoulders. Finally finished with that, he was in his car and pulling out of the parking lot, still grinning, when suddenly it all came back to him—the dance and the nomination and Ted and Cassi and all the hurt and pain and anger in his heart—and Moose knew instantly that the job as Santa had opened the way, truly opened the way. Now all he had to do was follow through.

"Oh, hello, Myron," Cassi said brightly as she answered the door. "Do come in."

Moose, as always, was struck dumb in Cassi's presence. His heart was racing, he could feel the red starting up his neck and striking at his ears, and he thought again of how he longed to be picking her up instead of her younger brother.

"You certainly look nice tonight," Cassi continued. "Who's the lucky girl?"

"Uh—there isn't a girl. Tonight, that is," Moose stammered. "Just Dan. Is he home?"

"He is if the amount of food consumed at the dinner table is any indication," she laughed.

Moose smiled. "Yeh, he's got a pit a mile deep. The tragedy is that he's so skinny."

"I'll say. It makes you wonder how the rest of us missed out, doesn't it?"

As he stood in the entranceway, Moose could hardly believe he was actually carrying on a conversation with Cassi. Maybe his dad *was* helping him.

"Myron," Cassi said, dropping her eyes but still watching him through her lashes, "did you hear about the contestants for king and queen?"

Dumbly Moose shook his head. Blast! Why did she have to spoil the moment by bringing up the dance? He'd have to tell her, and he didn't want to, not yet anyway.

"I heard there are now six contestants for king and queen. Three each. Can you believe that?"

"Yeh," Moose answered quietly. "I believe it. It'll probably change again, though. Things like that do."

Quickly Cassi looked up, wondering. Then, sensing that she might be digging a hole that neither of them would want to fall into, she hurriedly changed the subject. "You surely have a classy car, Myron."

"Yeh, it's nice."

"Nice? It's gorgeous! Dan told us it had been your father's, and that you've fixed it up yourself. Is that right?"

Suddenly feeling more secure about the direction things were going, Moose responded. "I don't know if it's right or not, but it's true. I either did it myself or traded for it."

"Traded? What do you mean?"

"Work," Moose responded. "I spent a lot of time at Leon Christensen's body shop, doing stuff for him to pay for parts and labor on my car. I—uh—don't have much money, but he was really super to work with me. I guess that's the *one* thing about being big that's okay. I'm pretty strong, and when I take hold of something, it generally moves."

Good grief! Moose thought frantically, why were his statements sounding so boastful? He didn't mean them that way.

"I can believe that, Myron. I—"

Just then the kitchen door was shoved open, and Dan hurriedly entered the room. "Let's go, Moose!" he shouted, grabbing his coat and swallowing the last of his supper. "Come on, or we'll be late! Leon said you couldn't use his shop past eight."

Moose stood still, his mind in a quandary. Should he tell Cassi or shouldn't he? Would it be better if she found out at school? Probably, but then he wouldn't be able to see her face, to see her reaction. And he wanted to see that, he really did. Only, what if the words wouldn't come?

"Uh—I'll be right with you, Dan. I've got to tell Cassi something first."

Both Cassi and her brother looked up at Moose expectantly, and the young man shuffled his feet, cleared his throat, and finally got it out.

"It's—it's about the Christmas Ball. I—I'm not running for king. I withdrew my name this afternoon."

"You what?" Cassi questioned, while Moose tried desperately to read the puzzled look on her face. "You withdrew?"

"Uh-huh. I really appreciated your nominating me, Cassi, but I got a job today, and I had to withdraw."

Earnestly Moose searched Cassi's face, trying to read her thoughts. Had she known what she was doing? Had she been part of the plot to run him against Ted, or had her nomination been a sincere expression of her thoughts toward him?

Oh, how Moose ached for an answer, any answer! If he could just know which way to go from here! He wanted so badly to ask Cassi flat out how much she knew, but he couldn't bring himself to do that. Not ever! Besides, her eyes were so sparkling and pretty that he couldn't see anything other than innocence in them.

"Uh—what kind of job did you get?" Cassi asked, and then she turned away from Moose's probing gaze.

"Oh, just a job."

"I know that, silly. But doing what?"

"Oh, mostly just — uh, talking to people."

"Clerking, you mean? Or sales?"

"Yeh, something like that."

"Do you need money so badly that you had to take the job *now*? I mean, after being nominated and all?"

"I truly do need the money," Moose answered honestly, "but there was more to it. Lots more, I guess."

Silence once again settled in the hall, where the three young people stood immobile. Dan's expression betrayed his own surprise at what he felt was Moose's gentle confrontation; Cassi's face was a study in various emotions; and Moose, his own face hopefully blank, was wondering how he was ever going to get out of the house. Cassi was innocent he thought — she had to be. No one could ever look so pure and be guilty.

"Uh — I've enjoyed visiting with you," he said to Cassi. "I guess I'll see you later."

Cassi smiled. Moose turned, opened the door, and led Dan out.

"How'd you find out?"

The question, from Dan, was asked when the roar of the buffer had finally subsided. Thoughtfully Moose rubbed the finish on the T-Bird with his hand, caressing the soft contours of the car's fender and feeling again the old pride in the vehicle his dad had set so much store by. He was certain he loved the car as much as his father ever had, and he was truly thankful that he'd had the time and somehow even the means to repair its wrecked frame and put it back in running condition. His father would be proud too.

"Moose?"

Surprised, Moose looked across the hood of the car to his friend.

"I'm sorry, Dan. My mind was wandering. What'd you say?"

"How did you learn of the nomination fraud?"

"Mr. Crockett told me."

"The counselor at school?"

"Yeh, he and I are old friends. He was even my bishop once. He said he didn't want me to get hurt any more than I already have."

Dan was silent, thoughtful, and when Moose turned the buffer back on he decided that the subject was better off left alone. Later, however, as Moose drove him home, spraying slush widely as he drove deliberately from one large concentration of melting snow to another, Dan decided that he had to know more.

"I wanted to tell you," he said carefully, not even noticing the stares from passers-by and his friend's erratic driving. "In fact, I had determined to do so, but I chose to confront Cassi beforehand so that my data would be complete and current and my arguments viable."

"Your arguments?"

"Yes. You see, I had hoped to persuade you to withdraw from the race. I—Moose, isn't this sort of thing a bit hard on your automobile's new finish?"

"Not really, except for the salt, and I'll get that on it anyway." Moose sprayed another pile of slush as he slammed into it. "Besides, it's fun, and I don't get much chance for that these days."

Dan watched his big friend, concerned but silent.

"Don't worry about the dance," Moose went on. "I resigned, just like I told Cassi. With my job, it seemed like the best and only thing to do."

"I believe you're right. By the way, you never did mention the location and nature of your employment."

"I'll tell you later. First, let me ask you a question about Cassi."

"Fire away, my friend of most voluminous size. I'll do my best to articulate any insight that my proximity to Cassi has given me."

Moose grinned. "Do you think she'll like the watch?" he asked innocently.

"Excuse me?"

"The watch, Dan. Do you think she'll like it?"

"Moose," Dan responded, his voice filled with incredulity, "that watch is undoubtedly the finest and most exquisitely designed example of a feminine timepiece I have ever seen. *Anyone* would like it. But surely you no longer plan on giving it to my *sister*."

"I do," Moose replied quietly. "It's more important now than ever."

"My friend, I think a combination of hormones, visual stimuli, and extreme loneliness has produced within your brain some rare form of insanity."

"Why?"

"Why? Didn't you see the guilt in her face? Moose, Cassi has treated you in a way that is less than sub-human. She deserves nothing like that watch, most especially from you, whom she has wronged so consistently and so thoroughly."

"Well, I think you're wrong, Dan. I think Cassi was sincerely trying to nominate me. Ted's the one who set it up otherwise. But even if you were right and she was involved, which I honestly don't believe, I'd still give it to her."

"You would?"

"Certainly. Otherwise there's too much to lose."

"Uh—would you care to elucidate on the perambulations of your mind?"

Moose took a deep breath. "Dan, giving that watch to Cassi is going to accomplish several things, though primarily it will tell her that someone other than Ted is interested in her. Somehow I have to let her know how I feel, and this will be the perfect way."

Dan was stunned, staring straight ahead. "You still like Cassi?" he finally asked. "After this, I mean?"

"I *think* that's what I've just been telling you, little buddy. Once she gets that watch, she'll owe me—"

"My friend," Dan interrupted, shaking his head as he spoke, "I think you're building castles in the air—dreaming, as it were."

"Possibly, but I don't think so. In any event, come Christmas day we'll surely find out, won't we?"

Moose suddenly popped the clutch and sped ahead, fishtailing around the corner onto Dan's street. "Fun, huh?" he asked innocently.

"You know," Dan said after carefully studying Moose's peacefully innocent countenance, "you are truly a most unique individual; a man among men, as it were."

"Yeh," Moose said, grinning ruefully as he braked to a stop in the Hancock driveway, "especially in size. But maybe after Christmas that won't matter anymore. Not, at least, if an expensive watch can do anything about it."

"Myron, could you please help me with the dishes?"

Moose, under the T-Bird and straining at an engine bolt with one of his father's old box-wrenches, muttered an answer but otherwise didn't stir. The car radio above him was playing "God Rest Ye Merry, Gentlemen," and the young man grinned as he watched his frosty breath spread up around the oil pan.

What a place to rest! he thought woefully. Anybody who'd do what he was doing had to be crazy! The temperature was below freezing, the concrete he was lying on was far colder than that, his old coat had a hole in it right where his left shoulder touched the garage floor, his hands were greasy and chilled, and all in all it was a pretty lousy place to rest.

"Come on, Mr. Bing Crosby," he muttered, "get serious. Who can rest during Christmas?"

Squinting his eyes he stared up at the engine, considering it once again. If he could just get all the bolts tightened, he reasoned, then the small oil drip would be eliminated. It wasn't bad, but still . . .

Carefully he fit the wrench up around another bolt and pushed. Nothing happened. He pushed harder, harder — and suddenly the wrench slipped off the bolt, Moose's knuckles smacked against the transmission case, and he yelped with pain.

"Doggone klutz," he muttered as he sucked his grimy and pain-filled knuckles, "can't you ever do anything—"

"Myron? Did you hear me?"

"I'm coming, Mom. Just a minute."

Still grumbling, Moose pushed the wrench against the bolt once more, crawled from beneath the car, wiped his hands on a dirty rag, and entered the kitchen. "Where's the dishtowel?" he asked, shrugging out of his coat.

"Right here," his mother answered easily. "Exactly where it always— Wait just a minute, young man! You're not touching this towel with hands looking like that. Merciful heavens, Myron, you're as bad as your father. I don't think. . . ."

Her voice trailed after a grinning Moose as he hurriedly went to the bathroom, washed up, and returned. He kissed his mother on the cheek and flew at the small pile of dishes. For a moment or so the two worked in silence, each enjoying the presence of the other, each occupied with his own thoughts, each inadvertently thinking of the same basic thing.

"So how is the election coming?" Mrs. Millett asked after a while. "Is my son going to be king?"

The question hung solemnly in the air, and Moose wanted desperately to ignore it. Instead of answering, he worked more quickly, hoping that his mom would forget she had asked.

"Myron, I asked you a question."

"Uh—I guess okay," he answered lamely as he put away a bowl he had just dried.

"Do you think you'll win?"

Moose took a deep breath. "No, Mom, I really don't. I think I was nominated as a patsy, so it isn't too likely that—"

"A patsy? What does that mean?"

Briefly Moose did his best to explain.

"Nonsense," his mother responded when he had finished. "People don't do things like that. You mark my words, Myron. You'll win, you hear? You will win!"

"Mom," Moose repeated determinedly. "Listen to me. I *can't* win."

"Why on earth not?"

"Because," the boy replied quietly, "I withdrew, tonight after school."

"You what?"

"I withdrew, Mom."

"But—but *why*?"

Moose looked down at his mother, and he knew he could not lie, not to her. But how could he ever make her understand what it was like, being a—a *moose*—a big nobody whose only purpose seemed to be to allow others to meet their own selfish needs? She just couldn't understand. She had always been so pretty and petite, and from her old yearbooks Moose knew that she had also been popular in school, something he didn't even know the meaning of. No, she could never understand! Maybe, though, he could somehow avoid telling her all the details.

"I just figured it was the best thing to do, for me, I mean. And besides, with my new job I don't think I'll have time to go to the dance."

"A job? You got a job? But why didn't you tell me?"

"Uh—actually I haven't had time. I just had my interview this afternoon. I'll be working at Maxwell's Department Store, and—"

"And so," his mother interrupted sternly, "you gave up the chance to be king of the Christmas Ball?"

Slowly Moose nodded, his eyes downcast.

"Son," his mother said quietly, "look at me, please."

Moose raised his eyes until he was looking down into his mother's face, and then she spoke again.

"Tell me about it, all of it. And don't try to spare me like your father always did. I'm tough, and I can take it."

Moose grinned in spite of his personal pain, and quietly he told her.

"I just can't imagine that boy, or anyone else, for that matter, setting you up," Mrs. Millett declared when he had finished. "Couldn't you be wrong?"

"No, Mom, I'm not. Someone set me up, and I'm so tired of everyone laughing at me that I decided to back out. The new job was a great excuse."

"Are you certain? How did you learn of this?"

Moose nodded again. "I'm certain. Mr. Crockett told me about it, Mom, and Dan confirmed it."

"Bishop Crockett? You spoke with him?"

"Yes, I did. He's the one who first told me."

"And do they truly laugh at you?"

"Sometimes it seems like it."

"But why? You're one of the kindest, most gentle—"

"Oh, come on, Mom!" Moose lamented, spinning away from her. "You know why. I'm huge, I'm clumsy, and they all think I'm a quitter as far as sports are concerned."

"But you left the team so that no one else would be hurt. Don't they know that?"

"They wouldn't understand, Mom. All those guys see is glory and winning and being better than everybody else."

"Does Cassi Hancock laugh at you too?"

"Yeh, sometimes, though I think it's because she doesn't know what else to do. Besides, I am kinda funny, and—"

"But laughing *at* someone? I just can't understand how young people who should be friends could possibly be so cruel."

"Mom," Moose replied gently, "they don't mean it that way. They're all good kids—except for Ted, that is. They just like to tease. Why, Cassi'd never hurt a fly, not if she knew about it. That's why I've got to help her get shot of El Numbskull Gomez."

Slowly Mrs. Millett reached out and touched her son's arm. "Myron, you are *so* like your father."

"Uh—Mom," Moose asked, knowing she was going to read something into him that wasn't there and wanting to forestall it, "can I share a secret with you?"

"Must you ask? Of course you can!"

Moose smiled and with one huge arm he hugged his

mother. "Well, I think I've figured out a way to get Cassi's attention."

Mrs. Millett sighed. "I don't understand you, Myron. Do you really like her that much?"

"I surely do, Mom. That's why I'm getting her a Christmas present."

Mrs. Millett looked up at her son, surprise illuminating her face.

"After this—this laughter, you're still going to buy her a gift?"

"Yes, Mom, I am."

"Myron, you are setting yourself up to get hurt."

"I don't think so," Moose answered slowly. "After she gets a gift this nice, then she'll have to—"

"Myron Millett, are you—are you trying to *buy* Cassi's affection?"

Moose looked down at his mother and wondered if he would ever get used to the feeling of being bigger than her. He couldn't remember having grown at all. He was always little, until one day quite suddenly he wasn't, and since then his growing just hadn't stopped. And the strangest thing about it all was that it still seemed like his mother was larger than he. In fact, near her he still felt safety and protection, and he feared her wrath just as he always had. Oh, if only she understood him! If only she knew what it was like to be a social outcast, to be laughed at all the time!

"I—I don't think so," he replied quietly.

"Didn't you just say it was your way of getting her to like you?"

"Well yes, but—"

"Myron, I'm ashamed!"

"But Mom—"

"My son, you are abusing that which is sacred, making a mockery of what a gift truly is, and I am ashamed. Even more, I fear for you."

"But—"

"Myron, didn't Jesus warn us about doing alms—in other words giving gifts—to be seen of men? Didn't Christ say that?"

Moose slowly nodded. For a moment the two stood in silence. Then Mrs. Millett reached up and took her son's face in her small hands and drew him down to her.

"Myron, my son," she said, her eyes moist with sudden tears, "I love you. I know that your father is proud of you, just as I am. I've never known anyone who had a heart so big and so filled with love. That you are able to see beyond Cassi's smallness is wonderful. But please, don't spoil it by a selfish smallness of your own."

Moose, embarrassed, felt his eyes start to flood over, and he would have turned away except that his mother pulled him closer and kissed him. And so he hugged her and remained silent, tearful and lonely, wishing with all his heart that things could be easy and simple, praying that once he gave Cassi the watch . . .

THREE

Department Store Santa

"A re you ready, Myron?" Mrs. Crockett stood at the door, impatiently waiting for her new Santa to follow.

Glancing at her, Moose marveled as he always did, wondering how anyone could seem so neat and attractive. Her striking blonde hair was perfectly in place, her clothing fit her well, her facial expression glowed with happiness and kindness, and frankly, she looked pretty as a picture.

He thought then of his own massive self, and of the trouble he had with his clothing and appearance. Making *anything* look good on his body was impossible, and this crazy red monkey suit was no exception.

"Myron, they're waiting. Are you ready to go?"

"Yeh, just about. Uh—are you sure these whiskers look real?"

"Of course they look real. And that Santa Claus suit fits you *perfectly!*"

Surprised, Moose looked again at her. Had she been
reading his mind? No, of course not.

"Now, hurry," Mrs. Crockett continued. "I'll go with you,
but I've got to get over to the toy department before . . ."

"I don't know," Moose muttered, delaying his inevitable
facing of the noisy crowd. He was deathly afraid, he was
sweating and his heart was racing, and though he didn't really
know why, he was doing his best to put off confronting all
those people.

What would he say, he wondered? Would all those little
kids laugh at him? He'd never been good at meeting people,
and he'd never been around kids at all. When he talked he
mumbled or stuttered, and— Oh good grief! Why had he
taken this job? What was he doing, thinking that he could be
a Santa?

"To me these whiskers look funny," he declared. "And so
does this hair. It's clear down past my collar, and—"

"Myron, put on those wire glasses. Quickly!"

Startled, Moose jumped to obey, dropped the spectacles,
breathed a sigh of relief when they didn't break, and finally
got them in place.

"Good." Mrs. Crockett smiled. "Now look in the mirror,
picture in your mind what you think Santa Claus looks like,
and tell me what you see."

Moose looked, and suddenly his face broke into a large
grin. "Well, I'll be—"

"Who is it, Myron?"

Moose turned, still smiling. "You know, this is weird. I can
hardly see *me* in there. That guy looking back at me looks like
Santa Claus."

"He is, Myron," Mrs. Crockett said gently. "*You are!*
Remember, once inside that suit you are no longer Myron
Millett. You are, literally, Santa Claus, jolly old Saint
Nicholas in the flesh. Furthermore, you will have no trouble,
once you start, in acting like him. You're hidden, and he's
visible, so just be who you see."

"But—"

"Myron, I mean it. From now until Christmas you will be the *only* Santa most of those kids out there will see. Just forget Myron Millett the moment you pass through this door. You are no longer him. You are now Santa—for the kids and their parents, for me, for the store, and I think most especially, for you."

Surprised again, Moose looked carefully into Mrs. Crockett's eyes. What did she mean by that? This was uncanny, strange as all get-out. How could she have known . . .

Mrs. Crockett smiled warmly and took hold of Moose's huge hand. "Now follow me, Santa," she said brightly. "The mob of anxious hopefuls is out there waiting."

And so, to the tune of an old record which was blaring over the store-wide speaker system—"Here comes Santa Claus, here comes Santa Claus, right down Santa Claus lane" —a fearing and trembling Myron Millett walked out into the cheering and whistling crowd of mothers and fathers and awe-stricken little children.

Being Santa Claus was not at all what Moose had expected. First, it turned out to be fun, which surprised him. Second, it was not embarrassing, but was instead very satisfying, and that was also surprising. In short, once he got past the fear of speaking with people, which was easy when he realized how hidden he was, Moose found himself enjoying his new identity more and more.

But that first day! What an unusual experience for an eighteen-year-old to have. Hundreds of kids sat on his lap, some willingly, some reluctantly, and many more were absolutely terrified. Some of the children were clean, others weren't, and a few were downright filthy. Some had lists a mile long, some had one single major item in mind, and more than a few simply couldn't make up their minds.

And the mothers and fathers were something else again. Some wanted photographs of their children with Santa, others

didn't. Some did all the talking for their children, others
wouldn't. Some forced their children to sit on Moose's lap and
grew angry when the children were afraid, others were very
gentle and compassionate. Some did a lot of yelling and order-
ing around, others were quiet and let their children make little
decisions on their own. Some were cranky from waiting so
long in line, others didn't seem bothered by it. And as with
the children, some were clean while others weren't.

In fact, after just a day or two Moose found that he could
look at the children, see the extent of their cleanliness, polite-
ness, loudness and kindness, and thus determine almost
exactly how their mothers or fathers would also be.

He also found, after the first few days, that he had become
the most popular Santa ever at Maxwell's. Not only was he
handing out more candy canes with each shift, but mothers
were making comments throughout the store that quickly
found their way back to Mrs. Crockett.

"Can you believe it?" she enthused at the end of a particu-
larly busy day. "Fan mail! From two mothers, no less! Moose,
do you by chance keep eight tiny reindeer at home? Who are
you really?"

Moose smiled, turned red, and said little. Mrs. Crockett
walked away shaking her head, and Moose resolved to be
even more the kind of person Santa Claus traditionally was.

It was fun for Moose to watch the children's faces, to feel
their shaking with fear as he lifted them to his lap, and to
sense their relaxing as he spoke with them and asked about
their Christmas desires.

He found quickly that the little ones usually wouldn't look
at him, and unless he could get them to do so, he could not
carry on a conversation. If they once looked into his eyes,
however, then they felt more at ease, so much so that some of
them even caressed his beard.

To get them to do that he devised little games, and one of
the best of those was played with a stuffed reindeer he got
from the toy department.

"Reindeer's gonna get me," he'd say, shaking the stuffed animal and softly ho-ho-hoing.

No response.

"Oh, no! Reindeer's gonna get me."

No response.

"Help! Help! Reindeer's gonna—" and then he'd whap himself gently on the head with the toy.

At that the children would always look up, he'd roll his eyes and repeat the process, sometimes also letting the reindeer sit on his head and then roll off, and usually by the third time through his little routine, the children would smile. Then he'd gently tap them with the reindeer, the grins on their faces would spread, and their hearts were his.

Moose noticed too that the mothers and fathers smiled at his silly game even more than their children. That, and the feelings of joy his success was giving him, gave him even more impetus to improve.

"I'm telling you, Myron," Mrs. Crockett said one afternoon as the young man prepared for his shift, "you have no idea of the good you're doing."

"How do you mean?" Moose responded.

"Oh, I wish I had time to tell you. Look at those kids out there, Myron. There're *hundreds* of them, and every day they show up earlier than the day before, just waiting for you. And the crowds of waiting parents keep getting bigger, too."

"Mrs. Crockett, that's just because Christmas is getting closer. I don't—"

"No, Myron, it isn't. I listen to them talk. Many of them are here because of you! Why, all day long I've been getting this place ready, trying to prepare for them. Just since ten o'clock I've had to supervise moving all the shoe racks back, and you wouldn't have believed all the dirt we found under them. Then there were the dresses in the women's clothing section—and I don't have time to talk about it because the toy department is in such a mess and I've got to go and get it cleaned up—but a whole rack of those dresses were summer styles, and I spent an hour with the salesladies trying to get that straightened out. Then Doug called me from home and he'd caught another mouse, and Robby, Jason, Ryan and Gregg all called me from every phone in the house and they wanted to go shopping and—well, have you ever had five sons? Of course you haven't, but can you believe it, they wanted to come here to Maxwell's. Why? To see *you!* I mean, to see Santa. They'd heard about you at school and were all excited because their friends said what a great Santa you were. Myron, we're already getting letters about having you here again next year. Can you imagine that? Just this afternoon I spent nearly *two hours* answering them, and besides that I had to go. . . ."

Grinning to hide his embarrassment but secretly pleased anyway, Moose sidled away and headed for his chair, ho-ho-ho-ing and patting little children on their heads as he went, wondering as he made his way through the crowd if Mrs. Crockett would ever run out of the millions of things she had to do.

So that was how Moose dealt with the tiny children. He learned as well that the ones who were a little older, say ages three or four through maybe seven, were actually very intelligent and communicative, and that fact surprised him. He had never had little brothers or sisters, but once he had learned that they were just little people, he more than made up for what he'd missed.

At first he had talked down to them, but that quickly ended as he found himself having some unique conversations, exchanges that showed him how innocently honest they were and how deeply they thought and felt about things. In fact, daily their thoughts intrigued and uplifted him, and he began to truly love them.

"Well hello," he'd say. "What would *you* like from Santa this year?"

"Where's Rudolph?"

"Uh—he's getting his nose ready for Christmas Eve, getting a brand new polish on it. What would you like me to bring you, then?"

"How do you do it?"

"Do what?"

"Get down our chimney."

"Uh—well, I usually—"

"It's a gas one."

"The chimney?"

"No, the furnace. Won't you get caught and burn up in there?"

Moose would grin and hug the child. "Merciful heavens, no! That's part of being Santa. Thank you for worrying about me, but you don't need to. I can get into all sorts of places, even without chimneys. It's sort of—uh—*magic*."

Or it might be:

"Hi. What would you like for Christmas this year?"

"Are those real?"

"What?"

"Your whiskers."

"Uh—well, yes, in a way. I—"

"Can I pull them?"

"Uh-uh! No way! You do that and you'll get whapped good, right where it'll do the most good. But you can touch—"

"I thought Santa was supposed to be *nice*."

"I am, but so's your mom, and I'll bet my whiskers against your loose shoelace that she whaps you sometimes. By the way"—and now Moose looked shrewdly into the youngster's face—"how many times has your mother had to whap you—*this year*, I mean?"

Eyes would quickly drop, Moose would hug the child, and then he'd take his big finger and lift the tiny chin until he was looking into sometimes glistening eyes.

"Hey," he'd say, "is that a smile I see coming? It sure is. Sure enough, there it is! Look at that happy smile! *That's*

what Santa likes to see. That's great! Now, what would you
like, more than anything else in all the world, for Christmas
this year?"

Grinning widely, the child would share his or her dreams,
kiss Santa's prickly cheek, and be joyously gone, leaving a
sticky but happy Santa watching them go.

So Moose's job quickly turned into something more than
work, and while he still feared exposure to his friends at
school, the young man actually found himself looking forward
each afternoon and evening to being Santa. The experience
exhilarated and lifted him, and every day he forgot a little
more the loneliness and humiliation that had been his.

One evening when there was an incredibly long line of
excited children and tired parents, Moose suddenly became
aware of a pair of dark eyes, large and very bright. They were
off to the side, behind his fence, they were set in the middle of
one of the cutest little faces he had ever seen, they were surrounded by wavy dark hair, and they were very thoroughly
taking the measure of his being.

Quickly Moose smiled and winked at her, but the girl,
who appeared to be about six or seven, only turned and ran.
Moose spent the remainder of his shift thinking about her.

Each day thereafter, as Christmas drew quickly nearer, the
little dark-haired girl appeared outside Moose's fence. There
was no regularity in her arrival time, and she was always
alone. Yet never once in all of those days did she come closer
than the outside of the fence. No matter what he said, Moose
could not entice the child to come and sit on his lap.

The young Santa worried at first that she might have been
an abandoned child, but he quickly decided against that. She
was always neat and clean, and though her clothing was
neither fancy nor expensive, she usually appeared well cared
for.

He worried too that she was out late and alone, and then
he noticed that she was always gone by eight o'clock. He also

noticed that occasionally she looked off behind his little house, as though she was keeping an eye on someone there. It had to be whoever was watching her, Moose decided, and that relieved his mind considerably. Still, no matter how many times she stood watching him, Moose could not coax her forward.

"Mrs. Crockett," he said perhaps three days after he had first noticed the child, "there's a little girl, and—"

"A little girl? Myron, there are a thousand of them out there, and maybe twice that many boys. I never *saw* such a crowd. And mothers? Good heavens, if each of them would buy just one dress— Do you know that just this morning—"

"Mrs. Crockett, she comes every day, but I can't get her to come sit on my lap. I've never seen anyone with her, and I'm sort of worried."

Mrs. Crockett looked up from her pin-neat desk. "You *are* worried, aren't you?"

Moose shifted his big feet uncomfortably. "Yes, ma'am, sort of."

"Myron, that's very sweet of you—to be concerned about a little girl you don't even know. I think I'm beginning to understand why Rod recommended you so highly, and why you're making such a fabulous Santa."

Moose stood silently, wondering about Mrs. Crockett's question. Did he? He'd not thought of that, but he was truly worried about that girl. He even thought of her at night, wondering what she was afraid of, why she wouldn't come to him. At school when his mind wandered it went to her, and he found himself trying to think of some new way to reach out to her, to get her to respond. But he could come up with nothing, and that was why he had come to Mrs. Crockett now.

"Myron, are you listening?"

Moose, embarrassed, focused in on the lady before him. "Uh—yes, ma'am. I'm sorry, but that little girl—"

"Of course. And Myron, I'm very pleased that you feel so

concerned about her. I don't often see that quality, even in mature adults. But I really don't think you need to worry. If she comes every day, she must be all right. Probably she lives near here, and sneaks in whenever she can."

"I've thought of that," Moose responded, his mind still worrying. "But that doesn't answer the question about why she won't get in my line. Why can't I get her to sit on my lap?"

"Oh, I'm sure she's just shy. But Myron, if anyone can reach her, you can."

"Well, before this job ends," Moose vowed as he walked toward the parking lot and his car, "that little girl will sit on my lap and tell me what she wants for Christmas. *That* is a promise, both to her and to me!"

The next two days passed quickly, and now it was the night of the Christmas Ball. Johnny Mathis was singing "Walking in a Winter Wonderland" over the p.a. system, and Moose found himself thinking, as he worked his way from one child to the next, not about the children and their requests but rather about the dance and about Cassi and Ted. Dan had told him they were going together, and he was certain they would be crowned king and queen.

For some reason beyond Moose's understanding, thinking of that had thrown his emotions into a tailspin, and he was truly having a hard time dealing with it. Again, as always, he thought, he had ended up the loser, while that rotten Gomez had taken all.

The big clock on the wall kept him informed of the time, and it was not difficult at all to equate the dragging minutes with the couple's presumed activities.

Now they were getting ready. Now Ted was picking her up. Now they were eating somewhere. And so on. Moose wondered who they were doubling with, and even *if* they were doubling. He wondered what Cassi was wearing, and he wondered what *he* would be wearing if he had taken her instead of Ted. Would Ted really be king, he wondered also, and would Cassi be queen? And how would it have felt if somehow it could only have been him as king, instead of Ted?

His thoughts turned then to Cassi and to the watch he was giving her, and Moose wondered for perhaps the thousandth time if the gift would accomplish all he hoped. He thought too of what his mother had told him, and remembering that brought out the guilt he was trying to bury.

Had his mother been right? he worried. Was it really wrong for him to use his gift to Cassi as a way to get her attention and to get her away from Ted? He considered again and again the idea of almsgiving that his mother had mentioned, and somehow it did not seem to mean quite the same thing as what he was doing. He wasn't giving Cassi the watch for praise, at least not the praise of men. He didn't want that at all. He just wanted her to know that he was alive, and that he was a real alternative to Ted Gomez. And how could that possibly be bad, especially when he was having such a negative effect on her? Besides, Ted deserved whatever he got.

But that was another prickly thorn in his conscience. If giving a gift in order to get Cassi's attention was wrong, then what did that mean about giving a gift as a means of seeking revenge? Moose didn't like to consider that question at all. So he pushed it aside and tried, really tried, to concentrate on the endless line of children.

"Ah, blast it all!" Moose muttered to himself as he helped a sticky and very dirty little boy down off of his lap. "Come off it, Moose. Remember you're Santa Claus, at least until next Wednesday night. Now act like it. Love these kids like they say you do.

"And as for Cassi and that watch, only time will tell you what good it will do."

Time?

Moose looked again at the big clock which hung suspended across the hall from him, and winced with jealousy; and as he helped a screaming little girl up onto his lap, his thoughts started all over again.

Ted was probably ringing the bell at Cassi's door just as he'd rung it so many times himself when he was picking up Dan. Cassi's mother was hurrying to open it just as she occasionally did for him. Cassi was coming through the door in a new formal gown, smiling beautifully like a true queen, radiating the quiet beauty only she could radiate . . .

Later, when the line of children was finally thinning and Ted was likely eating a formal dinner with Cassi in some fancy restaurant, Moose thought suddenly of the little dark-eyed girl. She wasn't anywhere in sight, however, so he turned back to the few children and parents who were left, ho-ho-ho-ing listlessly as he did so. He felt miserable, hated the thoughts of holding and listening to the few remaining screaming kids, and was wishing with all his heart that it was time to go home.

And that was when the group of teenagers came through the big front doors.

At first Moose was too stunned to react. They were kids from his school, seniors; they were dressed for the dance; and they were getting into his line! Frank and Allison, Mike and Suzi, Fenton and Carolyn—and *Ted* and *Cassi.*

Oh, no! How had they known he was there? Who could possibly have told them? And why were they there?

Moose died a thousand deaths as he did his best to listen to the remaining children. Yet the remarks of his classmates were easily loud enough to be heard above everything else. The couples were happy, obviously having a good time prior to the big dance, and as they drew closer Moose kept his eyes away from them, not wanting to see the excitement in Cassi's eyes as she clung to Ted Gomez's arm.

The moments seemed to drag on forever, but at last there were no children left. Time stopped, hung crazily suspended for several eternities, then rushed forward with incredible speed. Suddenly Carolyn was on Moose's lap with her arms around him, laughing, and Fenton was acting like he was jealous — only who could possibly be jealous of a store Santa. Carolyn was telling Moose how big he was, and then she was telling him that she wanted a new red Mercedes, and there was more laughter, and Moose was ho-ho-hoing emptily and giving her a candy cane, and then she was off to the side and Allison was on his lap flirting like crazy, and Frank was being silly too, and Allison also wanted a Mercedes, only blue instead of red, and . . .

And then to Moose's mind there came the thought of how unfair all this was, and of how rotten it was that he had been the one cursed with his immense bulk instead of Frank or Mike — or Ted! Yes, why hadn't it been Ted instead of him? Then Cassi would be hanging onto *his* arm and Ted would be the big oaf in the Christmas-red clown-suit!

Why was it always Myron Millett who had to be hurt, who had to be picked on, who had to give, give, give.

Moose hadn't planned on crying then, he really hadn't. It was just that he felt so low-down miserable, so deeply sorry for himself, that his eyes suddenly filled with tears. He didn't want to cry, of course, and he had no idea why it was happening, but the more he tried to stop it, the worse it became.

Fortunately Allison didn't notice, because at that moment she was making such a big deal out of her candy cane. But then, before Moose had time to do anything about his eyes or his emotions, Cassi was on his lap.

She too was smiling and giggling, and she was incredibly light, and her hands were held tightly in her lap just like all the other little girls held theirs when they were bashful and afraid, and Moose was wishing he had never taken the job though he was glad Cassi was on his lap, but it was all wrong, and she was saying that while the others might want Mercedes cars, she didn't, but instead she only wanted to be wearing a crown of some sort. And two tears slowly rolled down

Moose's cheeks and into his phoney white whiskers, and Cassi looked up just in time to see them. And when she saw his eyes she thought she recognized him, only she wasn't sure, and her own smile suddenly vanished.

"Myron?" she whispered in surprise, while the other kids continued their laughter and silly antics.

Moose blinked, two more humiliating tears escaped, and then Cassi did know.

"Hey, you guys!" she said, winking at Moose as she turned. "I know old Santa Claus here. He's my friend. In fact, he comes to my house all the time."

"Big deal," Allison jibed. "He comes to my house too. This year he's going to—"

"Allison," Cassi laughed, leaping to her feet, "stop being such an airhead. I mean, really. Can't you tell who this is?"

Moose, his face frozen with surprise, could not move, could not get up, could not even speak. Cassi was betraying him! Cassi! But it couldn't be true. She wouldn't do that, she couldn't. Not intentionally.

"Lemme see," Ted grinned, stepping forward. "I'll solve this little mystery of Cassi's. Okay, Santa, now it's my turn. Are you ready to hear what *I* want for Christmas?"

In that instant Moose might have stood, might have jumped up and walked away. He also might have seen Mrs. Crockett across the store watching, might have motioned to her for help, for support. But he didn't. He sat still and silent as he watched from behind his spectacles. Ted came forward, motioned for Cassi to leave, and then plopping himself on Moose's legs he threw his arms around his neck, ho-ho-ho-ing as he did so. And as Ted did his mocking imitation, Moose felt the red tide of anger washing upward through him, coursing, burning . . .

"Boy, you're a big Santa!" Ted declared as he pulled back and gazed into Moose's whiskered face. "Maybe you *are* the real one."

There was a chorus of voices, and no one even noticed the angry red flush that had already spread across Moose's face.

Under the mixed emotions of anger and frustration his tears were eliminated. This was the end! He had *had* it! A person could only stand so much!

Suddenly, with no clear idea of what he was going to do, Moose lunged to his feet. Ted, shaken from his lap, yelped, reached out to somehow catch himself, and grabbed hold of Moose's beard. A second later both tuxedoed youth and snow-white Santa's beard were on the floor.

"Why, you dirty. . . ." Ted snarled as he scrambled to his feet. "I'm gonna—" And then he attacked.

That at least was his intent, but something changed his plans. Suddenly he was on the floor again, his head spinning and his mouth filled with a strange sort of salty taste. With the back of his hand he wiped his face and split lips as he grimaced with pain, then he stared incredulously at the blood on his hand—his blood.

"Ted," Cassi was screaming, "don't—"

With a roar of anger Ted Gomez leaped to his feet and charged again, determined to teach Moose a lesson he'd never forget.

But as it turned out, a knee or a fist or something met Ted Gomez where he had expected to find a soft belly, and as stars exploded behind his eyes he went hard to the floor for the third time in only a few seconds.

Staggering to his feet again Ted was only dimly aware that a mountain named Moose Millett hovered above him like a red tank, hard, unscathed, his fists balled and tight, his face angry, his lips pulled thin.

Warning lights flashed in his spinning brain, Ted staggered back from the hulking menace, ducking the swing he knew was coming. And now a hand as large as a basketball had him by the shoulder, turning him, pulling him back, twisting . . .

And then a Kleenex was wiping the blood away, and Ted could see that Moose was holding it—though that made no sense. Then a lady was there, a Mrs. Crockett or something, a security guard was there too. Moose was telling them that Ted had fallen, and that everything was all right and that the group was just leaving. And then Cassi was beside him but was staring at Moose, and Mike and Fenton were helping him out of the store, and he was in his car; and for the entire remainder of the evening, even while he was in the royalty spotlight with Cassi, Ted Gomez worried about what had happened and what could possibly have done such damage to his face.

But Moose! he thought over and over again as he staggered along trying to follow Cassi's embarrassed lead. *Not Moose! Who in the world would have thought that a quitter like Moose Millett . . .*

And what about that Kleenex? Why on earth had Moose done that? Was it possible he had been wrong about Moose?

"Myron," Mrs. Crockett was saying as she stood beside the young giant back at the store, "what *happened*?"

Bleakly, silently, Moose looked down at her.

"Do you want to tell me about it?" she pressed.

Slowly the young man bent and picked up his beard, then carefully he fitted it back onto his face. "There's not much to tell," he finally said. "He got on my lap, and I got upset and dumped him off. I didn't really mean to, because he was in his tux and he was with Cassi, but he must have thought I did it purposely. Anyway, he came at me and I sort of lost my cool and . . ."

The young Santa paused and took a deep breath. "Well, I'm really sorry about that. Even if he had it coming, I shouldn't have hit him. Besides everything else, I broke a promise I made to my mom, and I—I— Oh, blast! I'm terribly sorry it happened here in your store, Mrs. Crockett."

For several seconds the woman regarded her Santa, seeing the pain in his eyes, the sorrow and humiliation burning in the expression on his face.

"Why don't we talk about it tomorrow," she said as she put her hand on Moose's arm. "Meanwhile, you go on home and get a good night's rest. Being Santa for all those hours, day in and day out, can be a pretty tough job."

Moose nodded but did not move. Mrs. Crockett squeezed his arm, turned, and walked away, and Moose watched her go, still without moving. Finally, when he was alone, he wiped the blood from his hands and turned back toward his chair, his brain numb, his heart aching.

And then he saw, staring at him through the fence, two dark and shiny eyes — eyes that were there, and then, just as suddenly, gone!

Moose sat in the Crocketts' living room, waiting for the counselor to get off the telephone. In the background of his mind he was aware of the one-sided conversation going on, but his thoughts were on the discussion he had just completed with Mrs. Crockett. He had apologized again, she had told him she understood, and suddenly he had felt that she, like her husband, truly did. Somehow that good woman actually knew what he was going through, and there was no recrimination over the fight she had witnessed the night before, no condemnation over Moose's outburst against Ted Gomez.

So now Moose sat silently, trying to decide what he should do, thinking about Cassi and her betrayal of the night before, worrying about it but not wanting to admit to himself that he was worried. He worried too about his gift to her, for no matter how he tried he could not get his mother's statement from his mind.

But did he believe his mother was right? Should he cancel the whole idea and just give up on it?

No! His plan was good, and he knew it. His mom just didn't understand. That was why she had declared her shame for him. But still, he felt he needed a second opinion, a supporting vote from people who understood him, understood what he was trying to do. And that was really why he had come to the Crocketts. They did understand, and they would support him. Of that he had no doubt.

"Well, Myron," Mr. Crockett said affably as he put down the telephone, "what brings you here today? Why aren't you out getting your Christmas shopping done?"

"I've been working on it. But I'm sort of worried about something, and I was hoping I could talk to you and Mrs. Crockett about it."

Mr. Crockett laughed. "Why not? We can tell you we don't know all the answers, just as easily as the next couple might."

Moose grinned, Mr. Crockett went out for his wife, and shortly the three were seated together.

Slowly then, and in as much detail as he could, Moose explained to the Crocketts his relationship with Dan Hancock and his sister Cassi. He told them how strongly he felt about the girl, how badly he felt because Ted Gomez was having such a profoundly negative effect upon her, and how intense his own desire was to win her away from Ted.

He did *not* tell them of the football incident and of his resentment toward Ted. That, he felt, was a side issue and wasn't part of the main problem at all.

"Anyway, like I told you at school, Mr. Crockett, I got Cassi a nice Christmas present, an expensive watch."

"Myron," Mrs. Crockett said, "that's really very thoughtful—"

"Let me finish, ma'am. I didn't buy Cassi a watch because she needed one, even though Dan says she does. Nor did I get it because I just wanted to get her a Christmas present. There were other reasons, and I don't even know if I can put them into words. But I really like her—more even than that, I guess —only she—she—well, I sort of thought if I gave her a gift like that, then she'd know how I felt about her and she'd sort of—well—she'd notice me."

"I see." Mrs. Crockett didn't move her eyes away from the young man who had become one of the most valued employees under her direction. Answers were always in the eyes, she had learned, if you could only understand what you saw there. Sometimes she could do that, and Myron's were so expressive, so open and gentle. Besides, she had seen something in those eyes the night before, a painful loneliness that had thoroughly surprised her.

Moose interrupted her reflections.

"Well?" he questioned.

Both Crocketts looked quizzically at him. "Well what?" Mr. Crockett retorted.

"Did I do something wrong?"

"Myron," the counselor replied, "I don't think I can answer—"

"Mr. Crockett, please. I need help. Mom quoted me a scripture about doing alms before men. It's in Matthew, I think. Anyway, she thought that's what I was doing. It doesn't seem like that to me, though. Actually I'm trying to help Cassi, and if in the process she starts to like me—"

"Whoa, Myron! Hold up! It isn't really as simple as all that, you know. Whether what you did is right or not depends on the things that are in your heart, and only you know what those are. To be honest, though, it certainly *looks* like you are using a gift to bring about your own purposes."

"I agree with Rod," Mrs. Crockett added, smiling, "but I'm certain it looks more like it to us than it does to you. You've heard the old saying that sometimes we get so close to the trees we can't see the forest. Maybe that applies here."

"Yeh, maybe. But honestly, even though I know I'll possibly benefit, I'm *really* doing this for Cassi's own good—"

"The end justifies the means, right?"

"Something like that."

"Myron," Mr. Crockett said gently, "I truthfully don't enjoy preachments, and so I hate to deliver them. But I want to respond honestly, and I know what I'd like to say is going to sound like preaching. Do you still want to hear it?"

Solemnly Moose nodded.

"Okay, here it is. Do you remember when you were twelve and you and your father came in for your priesthood interview?"

Moose nodded, wondering what that had to do with anything.

"You told your father and me that day," Mr. Crockett continued, "that your greatest goal in life was to please God. Do you remember that?"

Again the youth nodded.

"Myron, your statement truly impressed me, and I know it got to your father, too. In fact, we discussed it several times over the next year or so. But now I wonder, have you forgotten, or at least lost sight of, that goal?"

"I don't understand."

"Myron, in the premortal existence Satan wanted to use coercion. His doctrine was that the end justifies the means. God in his wisdom felt otherwise; he had given us our agency, the right to choose. Do you think your gift encourages Cassi's agency, or is it a form of coercion?"

"Mr. Crockett," Moose responded defensively, doing his best not to let his frustration turn to anger, "it's *only* a Christmas present!"

"Is it, Myron? Truly?"

There was a long pause, and Moose, his face red, stared at the floor. The Crocketts were just like his mother! Why couldn't anybody see what he was trying to do?

"Myron," Mr. Crockett suddenly said, "I can tell you're getting upset. Am I right?"

Moose grinned sheepishly. "Yeh," he admitted. "I am."

Mrs. Crockett reached out and placed her hand on Moose's arm. "Myron, it's difficult to hear one thing when we want very badly to hear something else. Rod and I understand your feelings of frustration, and your eyes tell both of us how sincere you are. Rod will stop if you'd like him to. Your friendship means too much to us to jeopardize it in this way."

Moose again smiled. "The guilty taketh the truth to be hard, right? I hate to admit it, but the shoe does seem to fit."

"Maybe not," Mrs. Crockett added quickly. "Maybe our view is distorted, rather than yours."

"Well, ma'am, I hope so. But whichever, I asked, and it'd be pretty silly not to hear you out. Go ahead. I'm listening."

"You're a good man, Myron." Mr. Crockett now hunched forward, leaning toward Moose. "Have you ever thought about gift giving as being sacred?"

Moose shook his head. "Not really. But since Mom told me about that almsgiving thing I've sort of wondered about it."

"Good point. If Christ thought it important enough to mention, it must be significant. Besides that, I'd like to tell you why gift giving seems sacred to me.

"The wise men gave their gifts to the Christ-child freely, with no thought of reciprocation. That was a shadow of what was to come. The Savior then gave himself as a sacrifice for us in the same way, completely freely. Our gifts to each other, especially at Christmas, should also be a type and shadow of those ancient gifts. They should be freely given, showing that we remember, understand, and appreciate Christ's gift, the Atonement. Doesn't that seem pretty sacred to you?"

Moose nodded thoughtfully.

"My mother, Zola Taylor, always said something that she had us children memorize," Mrs. Crockett interjected, again smiling her warm and encouraging smile. "It goes like this. 'In the eyes of the Lord, a true deed is done for the love of doing it; a plan is acceptable only when the welfare of another is the master thought; a labor is deemed worthy only when the sacrifice is greater than the reward; a gift is a gift only when the giver forgets himself.'

"Myron, let me ask you a very serious question. Does your expensive gift to Cassi qualify in any of these?"

Moose remained silent, his eyes dropped.

"Now, my friend," Mr. Crockett hastened to add, "don't take what either Kathy or I have said as absolute direction. Maybe your gift qualifies in all of the areas she just mentioned. You know your heart, and we may have misunderstood. I know that in at least *one* way your heart is good, and

I'm proud of you for that. I don't think *I'd* give a gift to Cassi, not if I had been in your place."

"But Mr. Crockett, she's an unusual person."

"I know you feel that way, and that's what I mean when I say you have a good heart."

"Mr. Crockett, I really don't think the plan was Cassi's idea. Besides, what about the idea of forgiveness?"

"Maybe you ought to give *Ted* the watch," Mrs. Crockett said, winking.

They all laughed, and then Mr. Crockett concluded. "I think you ought to know, Myron, that Cassi did plan the election thing—after her name had been submitted. She nominated your name *and* Ted's. She admitted it to Coach Nelson."

Moose listened numbly as Mr. Crockett continued, and it was a very somber young man who drove through the Christmas traffic a little later. Tears flowed unchecked, a giant heart ached, and still he turned the corner and steered toward the jewelry store where Cassi's Christmas watch was ready to be picked up.

For Moose, that Saturday afternoon shift as Santa was the hardest he'd ever put in. He couldn't concentrate on the children, he was extremely short-tempered, and he was so sour that even the little folks looked at him strangely when he ho-ho-hoed emptily at them. In short, he was a miserable young man facing a severe personal crisis.

Despite the mistake Cassi had made, Moose still couldn't really blame her for what she had done. She just wanted to be with Ted as badly as Moose wanted to be with her, and she was only trying to maneuver things so she could. It was no different from what he was trying to do, so how could it be all that bad? Good grief! No one was perfect, but if someone was close, it had to be Cassi Hancock.

That was why he was so upset over what the Crocketts had said. In a way they were right, but that didn't necessarily mean he was wrong. Even Mr. Crockett had admitted that. There was no black and white in the thing, only gray, and what was a person supposed to do with that? Still, there was a hollow feeling deep inside Moose that wouldn't go away, an uneasiness that was really making him miserable.

So all he knew for sure was that he liked Cassi and that— doggone it!—Ted Gomez wasn't good for her.

"Moose?"

It was break time, and Moose was in the employees' lounge, relaxing with a cold drink and doing his best to clear the confusion from his mind. Spinning at the sound of his name, he was shocked to see Ted Gomez standing in the doorway.

"Yeh?" he responded hesitantly.

"Have you got a minute?"

"Uh—I guess," Moose responded uncomfortably, wondering what on earth Ted was doing there. Looking down at his watch, he continued, "Five, actually. Come on in."

Ted came into the room, and with a start Moose realized that the athlete's mouth was all swollen.

"I'm sorry about that mouth," he said sincerely.

"So am I," Ted replied, grinning crookedly. "It hurts like the dickens."

There was an awkward pause. Ted took a deep breath, looked Moose squarely in the eye, and then spoke. "We missed you at the dance last night."

Moose, expecting anything but that, didn't know how to respond.

"Cassi and I won," Ted continued. "But the dance committee decided we should have a royal court."

"A what?"

"A royal court—for the yearbook, I guess. Besides, the voting was so close between me and you and Les Brown that —"

"Me? Ted, I withdrew."

Ted grinned. "I know that. People still voted for you, lots of them. You weren't there, of course, but Dave Clark read your name anyway, and you got the biggest applause of all. You are now a prince."

Moose was shocked to the core. Votes? Applause? Prince? How was all that possible?

"I told them," Ted went on, rubbing his jaw as he spoke, "that you were off being Santa Claus, but that I'd been in fairly recent contact with you, and that you had really made an impression on me . . ."

And then the two young men laughed, laughed in unison and with a comfort and comradery that Moose had felt with no one but Dan since his father's death.

"Uh—Ted," Moose said, "I—uh—need to talk to you, too."

Without sparing detail, Moose unloaded his guilt, apologizing to Ted for the things he had called him and for the jealousy he had felt toward him.

When Moose had finished, Ted followed suit, expressing his regret for the derisive comments he had been making, and also for his outburst of the night before. That led to Moose's explanation of why he'd left the football team. Each of the young men was just starting to re-evaluate his perspective of the other when Moose looked at his watch.

"Good grief!" he exclaimed, jumping to his feet. "I'm fifteen minutes late! Mrs. Crockett'll kill me! Ted, thanks for coming. I sure had you pegged wrong. From now on I'll . . ."

And Moose, in his haste to get out, accidentally kicked his chair, which skidded unerringly into Ted's left leg.

Both boys stared in surprised silence, then in unison they laughed again, shook hands warmly, and left the employee's lounge together, widely skirting the chair as they did so.

Later, when the last pint-sized hopefuls and their mostly tired and frustrated parents had finally gone, Moose groaned with relief, stood, stretched, and was just stepping down from his battered red throne when he saw, staring at him through the fence, the two dark eyes of his nameless little observer.

"Ah-ha," he whispered to himself. "I'll just pretend like I haven't seen her, and then . . ."

And so, unobtrusively, a giant red-suited Santa walked through the gate of his fence and, before the little girl could retreat, scooped her into his arms and marched back toward his gaily decorated Christmas throne.

FOUR

The Christmas Wish

"You know," Moose said gently as he sat down, "I've seen you lots, but you've never been on my knee. I hope you're not afraid of Santa Claus."

The small girl sat silently, her hands held tightly in her lap exactly like Cassi had held hers the night before.

"You don't have to be afraid," he persisted. "Santa loves little children. I'd never hurt anyone as sweet as you."

Still the child sat silently, her eyes downcast and her body rigid.

"Do you have a name?" Moose pressed. "I'll bet you have a nice name. All little boys have nice names."

"I'm not a boy!"

Pleased that the old ruse had worked, Moose looked down into the dark liquid pools of brilliance that were her eyes.

"You sure aren't a boy," he affirmed. "No boy could ever have eyes as pretty as yours. Will you tell me your name?"

"Rita Palmieri."

"Well, doggone!" Moose declared enthusiastically. "That's a beautiful name. How old are you, Rita?"

"Six."

"That's the best age there is. Rita, what do you want Santa to bring you this year?"

The little girl looked up at him, her eyes very clear and bright.

"You *aren't* Santa!" she said simply. "You aren't Babbo Natale!"

Moose could not hide his surprise, not at her statement but at her forceful candor. "What do you mean?" he asked quickly, knowing very well what she meant. "And who is this Babbo Nat—Nat—"

"Babbo Natale is Father Christmas," the child answered. "Momma says he's the same as Santa Claus. He's nice. I saw that big boy pull your beard off yesterday night, and I saw you hit him. Your beard's not real, and neither are you. Santa wouldn't hit *anybody*, no matter what they did! You aren't nice."

Moose took a deep breath and looked away. His mind was racing to find something he could say to her, some answer he could give this little child called Rita that would not hurt her. For some reason he felt drawn to her, always had since he'd first seen her eyes through the fence. But if she didn't believe he was Santa Claus, how could he talk to her? How could he discover anything about her?

"Well, Rita," he admitted finally, "you're right. I'm not Santa Claus. But I *am* one of his helpers, not a very good one maybe, but still I get to dress in this red suit like he does, and I'm proud to do that."

Rita looked up at him, totally silent, and Moose was suddenly very uncomfortable. It felt like the child was looking right through him, seeing all the weaknesses in his soul, evaluating him and finding him terribly in want.

"So if you'll tell me what you would like for Christmas," he continued, pushing his words out desperately, "I'll be sure and get the word to him."

Rita continued gazing into Moose's face, her eyes large and bright. Finally, however, she spoke. "Can you *really* talk to Santa? Even if you're not nice?"

Moose took another deep breath. "Rita, I usually try to be nice. I promised my mothe—mommy I would be. Last night I made a big mistake, and I—I feel very badly about it. But I won't do it anymore. Santa Claus knows that, and I think he'll still let me be his helper. Do—do you believe me?"

The little girl stared into his eyes and at last nodded solemnly.

"You do?" Moose asked in surprise.

Again Rita nodded.

"Good," the young man responded, grinning widely. "Now, what do you want me to tell good old Santa, good old Babbo Nat . . . Nat. . . ."

"Babbo Natale."

"Yeh." Moose grinned. "That's what I meant. What do you want Babbo Natale to bring you for Christmas?"

For long seconds Rita looked again at Moose, her liquid eyes boring deep into his soul, digging, prying, reading the deepest secrets of his heart. Finally, apparently satisfied with what she had found, the little girl responded.

"Can Santa *really* bring me what I want?" she asked.

Moose nodded. "He can surely try. He can't do miracles very often, but he's pretty good at solving most Christmas problems."

Rita's face instantly clouded, and Moose was amazed at how her eyes changed, growing almost smoky in color. "Then maybe he can't help me," she responded sadly. "Momma says that what we need is a miracle."

"Why? What on earth do you want?"

Again the little child looked up, and Moose knew she was not only sincere but sincerely troubled as well.

"I don't want anything for me, but could you tell Santa I need something very badly for my momma?"

Moose nodded. "You bet," he said quickly. "What is it?"

Rita looked down at her hands again, took a deep breath, and in her tiny voice she began.

"Tell him I know why he didn't come to our house last year," she declared, "and it's okay. Since my pappa left us we've moved a lot, and Momma can't talk good English, and I guess Santa just didn't understand how to find us. But we're here now, right behind this store, and I—I hope he can come this year."

"I'm sure he can," Moose answered quickly. "And when he does, what would you like, Rita?"

"Oh," the little girl answered quickly, a smile lighting her face. "It's like I told you. I don't want anything, not for me. Except, if he can find us, I wish—I wish he would help my momma to smile."

Moose gulped and looked once again at the little girl. "What?" he asked, thoroughly surprised. "No dolls, or *anything*? Wouldn't a doll make you happy?"

"Uh-uh," Rita declared firmly, shaking her head back and forth. "I'll never be happy again until my momma is. I know she's very unhappy, because she cries a lot, and when she cries, so do I. That's why I want Santa to help her to smile. I've already prayed and prayed about it. But nothing has happened, and I was hoping that maybe if I asked Santa Claus too, maybe all of them together could help me."

Moose had to gulp again. "You've even prayed about it?"

Rita nodded vigorously, her dark hair sweeping her cheeks. "That's why I *know* somebody's going to help my momma be happy this Christmas. If you could just tell Santa Claus about—"

"Don't worry," Moose interrupted, wondering as he spoke what he was getting himself into. If this was a Catholic family with marriage problems, then how on earth could he help?

And even if he could, *should* he try? He was a Mormon, he was just barely eighteen years old, and he was burdened with some pretty serious romance problems of his own.

"What would it take to make your mommy happy?" he heard himself asking, even while he worried. "Would—would she be happy if your daddy came home?"

"Oh, yes!" Rita quickly asserted. "But he can't."

"Why not?"

"Because he went away to live with Jesus and the Virgin Mary."

With his eyes suddenly swimming and his mind cursing the genes that had given him such fragile emotions, Moose hugged the little girl closely.

"He—he died?"

"Uh-huh, way last year. Momma and me miss him. We miss him lots!"

"I—I know how you feel," Moose said quietly. "That's where my daddy went as well, to live with Heavenly Father. And I miss him too. Very much."

Rita's eyes were again large and deep and clear. "You're pappa's dead?"

Moose nodded.

"Does your momma cry?"

Again Moose nodded. "Yeh, and so do I. When fathers or mothers die its awful lonesome. I cry mostly at nights."

"That's when my momma and I cry, too."

For a moment both Moose and the child were silent, thinking.

"Rita," he asked carefully, "if Santa Claus can help you, what does your mommy want that will make her happy?"

"To go home to Grandpapa and Grandmama," the girl stated with certainty. "Momma doesn't have a job, and she says she's awfully lonely here."

Warning bells jangled in Moose's mind. Rita had a kind of accent, so he could see it coming, and knew that when it did he'd be lost, without any way to help. Still, almost as if it was coming from outside of himself, he heard his voice asking where Rita's grandparents lived.

"In Italy," the child responded innocently.

Italy! Moose's mind reeled.

"Can't she call them? On the telephone, I mean?"

"No. Mommy says we can't afford a telephone. Maybe if she gets a job, then we could get one."

"Sure. Then you could call them once in a while, and she wouldn't be too lonely."

"Uh-huh. Momma'd like that."

"Is there anything else your mommy would like?" Moose asked quickly. "To make her happy, I mean?"

"Uh . . . I don't think so."

"Then how about something she needs? Could Santa bring her something like that? Clothes maybe, or food?"

"Well, she's cold a lot. Maybe she would be happy if she had a coat."

"Okay," Moose interrupted, thinking quickly. "Coats do help people that are cold. Somehow, I *know* Santa will help."

Moose paused, looking down at the little girl on his lap. "Now Rita, Babbo Natale really worries about little girls like you."

"He does?"

"Oh, yes. He worries because you've been awfully unselfish, and he'll feel bad if he can't give you something to show how proud of you he is."

"Really?" the child asked, her eyes getting even wider.

"Absolutely. Now what would you like him to give *you*? Besides your mommy's happiness, I mean."

"Well," the little girl declared thoughtfully, "I don't want Father Christmas to feel bad. But I don't want anything for me! Honest-cross-my-heart and hope-to-die I don't! This is my momma's Christmas."

"Rita, Christmas is for *children*, not their mommies and daddies. Isn't there something — ?"

The little girl's response was quick and firm. "Uh-uh!

Christmas is for everybody, 'cause Jesus was for everybody, and Christmas is his birthday! Momma says my pappa said so!"

Moose stared, more than a little surprised at the tiny girl's response. She was right, of course. She even sounded like Bishop Crockett and his wife. But how could she know all that? She was just a little girl!

"Nothing for you?" he repeated once more, his mind also grappling with the small girl's determined and totally selfless statement. "Are you sure?"

Solemnly the little girl nodded.

Moose squeezed the child again. "Okay," he sighed. "Come on. At least I can walk you home."

Hand in hand the red-suited young man and the tiny dark-haired girl left Maxwell's Department Store.

For hours Moose lay in his bed, unable to sleep. He tossed and turned, he prayed, he tried to have a conversation with his father, he even thought of Cassi and of his unusual conversation with Ted. But it was all useless. No matter how he tried or what he did, he couldn't get little Rita and her amazing statement out of his mind.

"I don't want anything for me. I don't want anything for me. I don't want anything for me. I don't want anything . . ."

Over and over the declaration played in his thoughts, repeating itself like a broken record. The only difference was that records being played maintained a steady volume. His mind, on the other hand, seemed to be steadily increasing the decibel level at which he heard the phrase . . .

"*I don't want anything for me.*"

Finally Moose could take it no longer. He threw back his covers, crawled from his bed, and strode to the window. For a few moments he watched the snow, which again was falling. At last, his mind made up, he opened his door, crept down the hall, and paused at the doorway to his mother's room.

"Mom," he whispered. "You awake?"

"Uh—Myron, is that you?" Mrs. Millett answered after a moment's hesitation.

"Yeh. Are you awake?"

"Well," she responded, smiling into the darkness, "I am now. What do you need?"

"Uh—can I talk to you?"

Mrs. Millett rolled over, turned on the light, and motioned for her son to come sit beside her on the bed. He did, and then for several seconds there was silence.

"Mom," he finally said, "I have a problem."

"Cassi?"

"Well, yes and no. Actually I have two problems, but for now Cassi is the second one."

Mrs. Millett wisely remained silent, watching her son, feeling thankful that her many prayers seemed finally to be bearing fruit.

"You were right about my reasons for giving Cassi the watch," Moose said, finally breaking the silence. "I guess I was just too stubborn to see it."

"I hoped you'd understand."

Moose laughed without humor. "I'm glad I did. But I'll tell you, it took a lot to get through. Even the Crocketts tried to tell—"

"Bishop Crockett?"

"Yeh, I went and talked to him and Mrs. Crockett. I guess I wanted them to tell me I was doing a good thing. Instead, they really laid it on me."

Mrs. Millett smiled. "Well, I'm thankful you listened to *somebody*."

"Mom, what they said just made me more determined than ever to go through with my plan."

"I—I'm afraid I don't understand. Why did you change?"

"It was a girl, Mom. That's what I want to talk to you about. She's a tiny little thing with big black eyes and a smile that would melt an iceberg. Her name's Rita, and I just talked to her tonight over at the store and she knew I wasn't Santa

Claus because she'd seen Ted pull off my beard the night before and she'd also seen me hit him and I told her how sorry I was about it all, just like Ted and I told each other today, and—"

"Myron! Slow down! Is this Rita a new girl friend? And what about Ted? What happened between you and him? I don't even know—"

Moose, so abruptly stopped, grinned. "I'm sorry, Mom. Sometimes I just get excited. She's not a girl friend, because she's only six, and I'll tell you all about Ted and me another time. Anyway, what this little Rita said really got to me, and I can't clear the tape. It's in my mind and it won't go away."

"The tape?"

"Yeh—you know, like a recording. Over and over I keep hearing her say it."

"Yes?"

Moose smiled. "She said, 'I don't want anything for me.' Mom, can you believe that? She *really* didn't want anything! She's the only kid who's been on my lap this whole Christmas season who hasn't asked for something for herself. And she meant it, too. All she wanted was something for her mother."

"My goodness," Mrs. Millett exclaimed. "What an unusual child! No wonder you can't get her out of your mind."

"I'll say! The funny thing is that suddenly it's all so clear, this business of true selfless giving. You tried to tell me, the Crocketts did the same, and then somehow that little girl got through my thick skull."

"I'm happy for you that she did," Mrs. Millett said softly. "But I still don't see the problem you mentioned—"

"Well, I have this great idea, Mom, and I don't want you to get upset when I tell you about it. Okay?"

"Myron, why should I get upset?"

"Well, 'cause we don't have a whole lot of money, and this is going to be sort of expensive. I want to give Rita and her mother their Christmas. I've been *playing* Santa for almost four weeks. Now I want to do it for *real*!"

"Why, that's wonderful! Have you earned enough at your job?"

"I've done okay. It'll mean my Christmas to you will be a little thin, but —"

"So that's the problem," Mrs. Millett replied, laughing. "Myron, you know I don't need —"

"Mom, that isn't it. You see, they're Catholics."

Mrs. Millett looked at her son in surprise. "So?"

"Well, I mean, we're Mormons, and I didn't know if you —"

"Myron, for heaven's sake, aren't we all God's children?"

"Well, yes, but we usually try to help someone in the ward, and —"

"Then your big problem is no big problem at all. If she needs help, of course you should do it. I'll help, and — Myron, why are you smiling?"

Moose's grin spread wider. "Mom, I *knew* what you were going to say. Thanks for — for just being my mom."

Leaning over, Moose kissed his mother gently. For the next hour the two of them planned what they would need to do.

"Hi, Myron."

"Hi, Cassi. Is Dan home?"

"He certainly is. Come in, please."

Moose stepped quickly into the entryway of the Hancock home. "Sure snowing," he said lamely.

"I noticed."

There was a heavy silence. "Would you like to sit down?" Cassi asked at last.

"No thanks. I'm all wet, and . . ."

Silence again, thick, strained. Moose stared at the floor, wondering at how his heart was beating, worrying that Cassi might hear it and grow alarmed. She was so lovely.

"Myron, I — uh — I'm so glad you're part of the Christmas royalty."

Moose looked up, smiling slightly. "Yeh, that was a surprise, wasn't it. Uh—for me, I mean," he quickly added.

Good grief, he thought to himself. *Why did I say something like that? She'll interpret it wrong and feel badly, and I hadn't meant it that way at all. Her expression looks stricken.*

"Myron?"

"Huh?"

"Uh—oh, gosh! Never mind. It's nothing." Cassi started blushing, and hastened to cover it. "Just a sec and I'll get Dan."

She smiled briefly and was gone, and Moose was left alone, wondering, feeling terrible, and still thinking of how beautiful Cassi Hancock truly was.

"Moose, you can't!"

"Maybe you're right, Dan. But I've *got* to try."

Dan was totally exasperated, but Moose was involved again with the air-wrench, removing another tire. The racket in the STANCO station was deafening, and Dan fought the urge to hold his hands over his ears.

"No, you don't!" Dan declared when all the lugs had been removed. "Such an idea is implausible if not absolutely impossible."

"Dan," Moose responded gently as he eased his wheel onto the wheel-balancing mechanism, "nothing's impossible. That's what Dad always said, and I believe it. Somehow a way will open up."

"Well, I'll have to admit that for you, at least, things seem to do that. There is one question, however, that continues to perambulate around pretty freely in the gray matter wherein my mental gyrations occur."

"What's that?" Moose asked as he started the wheel spinning.

"It's nothing significant. I was just wondering where you plan on getting the moola, the dinero, the argent, the scratch. You know, the dollars. Women's clothing isn't cheap, you know. I've watched Cassi go shopping, and it about drives my father crazy."

"I know it isn't cheap," Moose replied quietly as he marked the spots where the weights were needed. "And I *don't* know where I'll get the money."

Efficiently Moose pulled the wheel off the machine and began tapping weights onto the marked places on the rim.

"Where did you learn this skill?" Dan asked, intrigued.

"Stan Pope taught me. He's the owner here, and he's a great guy. I pump gas for an hour or so a week, and he lets me do this in trade. Here, let me get past you, Dan. Uh— good! Now hand me those lugs."

"Those how much?"

"The lugs, Dan. Those five metal things there in the hubcap. Good. Now hand me the air-wrench . . ."

Dan did, and once again the horrible racket filled the otherwise empty station. Dan shook his head sadly, concerned about his friend's ambitious idea. Finally, when Moose was spinning his next wheel, he gave Dan another shock.

"One thing I'm going to do, Dan. I'm going to ask Ted Gomez for his help."

Speechless, Dan just stared. "Moose, sometimes even my phenomenal mind has difficulty grasping your mental cogitations! Why?"

"We had a good talk last night, and . . . Well, I think he's an okay guy. In fact, I really like his style."

"Oh, I understand. The prince thing. You're changing your mind simply because you're in the royal court with him. My friend, I am distressed. I always thought you had more sense—"

"Hey, little buddy, hold on. Trust me a little, will you? I've been pretty hard on Ted, and I'm just looking at things from a different angle."

"What about my sister?"

"What about her? I think she's one of the neatest people in the whole world, not to mention one of the most beautiful. I can't believe how the very sight of her throws my heart into overdrive, but it surely does."

"Then what about her and Ted?"

"Tragic, isn't it?" Moose grunted as he lifted the wheel back into place on the T-Bird. "But let's not worry about it now. From you, little buddy, I need just one thing. Beyond your friendship and vocabulary, that is. Promise me that you'll be available Christmas Eve. My sub-for-Santa project is going to need all the help it can get."

"Don't worry, Moose," Dan replied, trying to clear the confusion from his mind. "I wouldn't absent myself from such an event for anything."

"Good. And one thing more. Could you bring a car? Mine'll never hold all that stuff."

"Sure. It's about my turn to drive anyway, so I'll just borrow my father's Caddy. Should I meet you at the store?"

"Yeh. Unless I call you, be at the back door at six o'clock sharp. That's when we close for Christmas Eve.

"Oh, by the way," Moose continued, changing the subject. "I have Cassi's Christmas present here. Can you smuggle it in under your tree for me?"

Dan looked shocked. "My friend," he cried. "No! I thought you had changed your mind. I thought you had determined that such a course was unwise, unprofitable—"

"Dan, just do it. Please."

"Well," the younger boy responded, "I don't know . . ."

But Moose smiled and squeezed his friend's arm. Dan winced and then grinned, and the deed was good as done. Cassi's Christmas was delivered.

The next three days were very busy for Moose, but very satisfying as well. At last, he felt, he had the true Christmas spirit. He'd spent several hours with Ted, who'd agreed to help, and things were well on their way.

In addition, Moose found that his experience as Santa had grown even more rewarding. More children enjoyed his enthusiasm, more mothers and fathers commented to sales clerks on the extraordinary Santa they had hired, and as the feedback reached him, Moose gained an even greater desire to excel.

"Myron," Mrs. Crockett said on the afternoon of the twenty-fourth, as he came in to suit up, "it's absolutely remarkable what you have managed to accomplish. I don't think any other employee has ever impressed Mrs. Maxwell like you have. Did you know that she was here last night, watching you?"

Shocked, Moose started to color. "Wh—where was she?"

"Over by the lingerie. And what a mess that was. The whole department looked like a herd of elephants had romped through it. I saw it about thirty minutes before Mrs. Maxwell arrived, and you never saw anybody flying around like those clerks and I. Every table had to be refolded, the racks moved, and so on. What a mess!

"Anyway, she came specifically to see you. One of her neighbors has been in here twice with her children, and she's never stopped talking about you. So Mrs. Maxwell came to see her very own store Santa."

Moose looked up when Mrs. Crockett paused. "Well," he finally asked, thanking his lucky stars that the old lady had chosen the previous night instead of the Friday or Saturday before, "what did she think?"

"Myron, she *loved* you."

"But—but why? She didn't even talk with me."

"She talked to half a hundred mothers and children, and she probably sold every one of the mothers at least one item of clothing. No grass grows under that woman's feet, even if she is in her eighties. Anyway, her comment to me this morning was that it was too bad we couldn't use a Santa all year long."

"Yeh," Moose grinned, "that'd be great. My wallet would love it too."

"And Myron," Mrs. Crockett continued, apparently not hearing him, "she's very perceptive. She knows you enjoy it as much as you appear to. That alone impressed her immensely."

Moose, embarrassed but pleased, mumbled his thanks, excused himself, and walked away, not even seeing the knowing smile Mrs. Crockett flashed after him. Nor, for that matter, did he learn the great news she had not yet delivered, the news which she had suddenly decided would wait until Christmas morning—in an envelope under his tree.

It wouldn't have mattered a bit if she had told him, however. Moose was too excited about what he was doing, too involved with little Rita and her mother. Such tidbits of information as Mrs. Crockett might have told him, tidbits concerning a raise and permanent employment, were trivial indeed compared to what he was truly doing.

And that, of course, was being the sort of Santa Mrs. Maxwell loved.

"Why did you want Dad's car, Dan?"

Quickly the boy looked at his older sister, wondering how much he dared tell her. Almost all, he quickly decided. After all, what could it possibly hurt?

"Moose has a Christmas commemoration coming up tonight on Harris Street right behind Maxwell's; he has implored me for aid; and because he needs more space than his own car can provide, he has requisitioned my assistance."

"Dan," Cassi responded with a sigh, "I wish somehow you had learned to speak normal English, instead of whatever it is you and Dad speak. Tonight both of you are talking riddles. I really think your thesaurus has ruined you. Now what sort of 'Christmas commemoration' is it *you* are speaking of?"

Dan grinned. "You know, sis, if you maintain a close association with Father and me for a lengthy enough period of time, there may yet be hope for your grammar deficiencies."

"Come on, little brother. Knock it off and tell me."

"It seems to me that you are exhibiting a rather unusual interest in my large friend. Can such an assumption be true?"

Cassi groaned. "Dan, you're too much. Besides, I've always thought of Myron as *my* friend, too."

"*Myron*, is it? Wow! Wait until Moose hears of this."

"I've always called him Myron, you dipstick. Just ask him."

"I just might," Dan responded. Then, with a thoughtful look, he continued. "You know, Cassi, Moose might be right. He just might, at that. He swears consistently that you are wonderful."

Dan paused, looked long at his older sister, thought of saying more, and decided abruptly against it. "Well," he declared, "I must bid thee farewell, sweet sister. My abundantly built friend will be ready in a mere twenty minutes."

Without waiting for a reply Dan turned and departed, and Cassi, deeply troubled, dropped onto the sofa and stared out into the darkness of early evening.

FIVE

Gifts

For as long as he lived, Dan knew, he would never forget that Christmas Eve. It started off at Maxwell's, where he, Ted Gomez, and a Santa Claus-suited Myron Millett loaded a huge pile of packages into the Cadillac.

"My word!" Dan groaned as he gathered up another armful of brightly wrapped packages. "I am astounded by the sheer volume of gifts."

Ted, staggering under a load of his own, agreed. "Moose, I've got to hand it to you. This is some kind of Christmas. You've really done a number for that family."

"Not me," Moose responded as he gathered up a load himself. "When Mrs. Crockett found out what I was doing, she went wild. She's the one who did it. I'd told her about little Rita, and when she saw her, well—I mean, look at this. I think she's talked Maxwell's employees into wrapping up half the store."

Dan was even more surprised. "They *all* contributed to this endeavor?"

"Not quite, but nearly. I got some stuff, Mom and I together selected the coat, and the rest of this came from folks here in the store. That Mrs. Crockett's really something! She had the word out in twenty minutes, and within another twenty, packages started piling up here by the door. I guess almost every employee contributed—"

"Contributed?" Dan asked. "You mean these things aren't surplus, or extras, or—or . . . My heavens, do you mean to imply that the employees *paid* for these things?"

"What'd you think they'd done?" Ted questioned humorously. "Stolen them?"

Moose laughed a little, and Dan looked sheepishly from one boy to another. "I—I don't know," he responded. "I just cannot imagine all this. I suppose I thought that somehow the store, or Mrs. Maxwell, or—"

"To be honest, Dan, I doubt Mrs. Maxwell even knows about it. Mrs. Crockett only let the word out yesterday, and I don't think she's been in since then."

Moose stacked an armful of packages into the back seat of the Cadillac, turned, and began taking more gifts from Dan as Ted returned to the store. "You know," he continued, "ol' Ted is a good man. Do you know that in the past two days he and I have visited every senior boy in the school?"

Numbly Dan shook his head.

"It's true, Dan. He convinced me that this was too good a thing not to let them in on it. Each boy gave what he could, and we came up with a little over $160.00 cash. Not bad for a couple of heavyweights, I'd say. And to think I used to call him El Creepo Gomez. I can hardly wait to—"

"Hi, you guys."

Both young men spun around as Ted came through the doorway with more gifts. All three were equally surprised to see Cassi Hancock standing on the sidewalk behind them.

"Hi, Cassi," Ted replied, while Moose and Dan just stared. "How did you ever find us?"

"Good detective work," Cassi answered with a smile. "Dan mentioned that Myron and the store were involved with something on Harris Street, so here I am."

"Hey," Moose responded, "we're glad you're here. We're almost loaded, and it'd be great if you could come to the Palmieri home with us."

"That's right," Ted agreed quickly. "We could really use your help. Sort of a 'beauty and the beasts' type of thing."

Cassi, feeling more than a little nervous and embarrassed, smiled again.

"I appreciate the offer, you guys, and I'd love to help. But Dad's in a hurry for his other car, so I've just got a sec. Knowing Dan like I do, I decided all of you would be hungry. Here's a little munch food from McDonalds."

From behind her, Cassi revealed a large sack of food, which she handed to Moose.

"Hey," the red-suited giant declared as he took the food, "this is great! And so are you, Cassi. This is really very thoughtful of you."

"Yes," Dan quickly agreed. "For a sister who never admits that she eats, you've done very well."

Everyone grinned, and suddenly the silence became strained and awkward.

"Uh — M — Myron," Cassi finally stuttered, "the real reason I came was to — uh — speak with you."

Moose stared, a knot of fear beginning to form in his stomach.

"Is this a private conversation?" Ted asked.

"As a matter of fact, Ted, it isn't. I'd like both you and Dan to stay, since in a way we're all involved.

"Myron," she plunged on, "I — I've had a pretty unpleasant month since I nominated you for king, and if I could ever live December over again, I'd do it in a minute."

It was difficult for Cassi to tell who was more nervous, her or the three boys who stood facing her. Somewhere out of sight a car honked, there was a brief sound of tires plowing through wet slush, and then all was still. Cassi shivered and wished with all her heart she had never thought of the idea to nominate Moose.

"I know you found out about our plan, Myron, because you withdrew."

"My withdrawing didn't work very well." Moose grinned awkwardly.

"I'll say," Dan agreed. "Now you'll all be in the yearbook together. Talk about a convoluted entanglement of semi-amorous involvement."

Moose, Ted, and Cassi exchanged looks, all smiled awkwardly, Moose grabbed Dan by the neck and shook him teasingly, and then Cassi continued. "Anyway, Myron, that whole thing was my idea, and I'm deeply sorry. I—I don't think I've ever stooped so low in my life."

"Aw!" Moose scoffed, wanting desperately to lighten Cassi's burden. "It wasn't anything serious. Besides, you did me a favor. Ted and I have talked some, and a whole lot of things have been cleared up. In fact, I feel better about things now than I've ever felt."

Cassi smiled up at the large young man. "Thanks, Myron. I know what you're doing, and you're very sweet. Dan, with all his vocabulary, has never managed to exaggerate when he's described you."

"Wait a minute," Dan declared. "My vocab—"

"And you know what else?" Cassi continued, interrupting her younger brother, who wisely grew silent. "I think I won that royalty contest so that I could have even more pain, realizing what I had—had done—to you. I honestly have never felt such shame and guilt."

"We've both felt it," Ted added. "I don't know why people do such dumb things, but about every other day my mother

says she'll be glad when I grow up. To tell you the truth, so
will I. I just hope it helps."

"Myron," Cassi concluded, her eyes pleading earnestly,
"will you please accept our—*my* apology?"

Moose, embarrassed, looked down. "Sure," he replied
quietly. "I—I never did think you meant anything mean,
Cassi. I told Dan I felt like I—I understood."

There was silence again. Down the street a dog barked.
Cassi looked at her watch.

"Good heavens!" she cried. "I was supposed to have Dad's
car back ten minutes ago. Have fun, you guys. I wish I was
going with you."

With that, Cassi climbed back into her car and sped away,
and three thoughtful and very hungry young men looked at
each other, grinned, and together attacked a mountain of Big
Macs and fries.

Not many minutes later the same three young men, their
stomachs and hearts full, stood on a small and dilapidated
porch. They could hear the radio in the home playing softly,
but other than that there was no sound. Suddenly Doris Day
started singing "Toyland," and Moose grinned.

With Ted on his right and Dan on his left, Moose loomed
almost larger than life, and Dan realized once again how truly
large his friend was. In one arm Moose held a tree, in the
other were decorations for it, and he still didn't seem
encumbered.

Ted too was loaded down, and Dan could hardly believe
that he was standing there with those two giants of the school.
What luck! It was more than a mere junior could hope to ask
for, he concluded, the association with men like these, the
intellectual stimuli it afforded.

Dan, who held several packages himself, realized that his
heart had never pounded so wildly. How would the woman
respond, he wondered, and what would he say to the two
strangers when the door opened?

Moose always seemed so tongue-tied, Dan thought; Ted

didn't know these people at all; and very few could understand Dan's own vocal efforts either. So who would be their spokesman? It was too bad, Dan mused, that Cassi could not have stayed. She certainly seemed to have an easy way with words.

Of course, Moose seemed to become an altogether different person when he was dressed as Santa, and his vocal conduct with Cassi and Ted had been impressive. Perhaps he could handle it.

Suddenly the door opened and a tiny dark-haired woman was standing in the doorway. She started to ask what the visitors wanted and in that instant was overwhelmed by the sight of the giant Santa Claus.

She gasped as she stepped back, a startled look on her face. "*Babbo Natale*, can it be? Are you truly Father Christmas?"

And then a voice neither Dan nor Ted had ever heard before boomed out from the red-coated figure above them.

"Ho-ho-ho." Moose laughed heartily and with genuine pleasure. "Merry Christmas, Mrs. Palmieri, and may your holidays be filled with wonderful things. May we come in?"

The poor woman was stunned, and she was still staring upward when tiny Rita rushed past her mother and squeezed Moose's leg.

"I *knew* you'd come," she squealed as she jumped up and down. "I told Momma you would, but she didn't know, and —Oh, Momma, look! A *tree!*"

Moose, somehow picking up the little girl along with everything else, pushed gently past Mrs. Palmieri and into the house. Then, knowing that they had probably remained unseen, Dan and Ted shouted "Merry Christmas" in unison and carried armloads of gifts into the small home as well.

As though he had done it every day of his entire life, Moose swiftly set about decorating the tree, laughing the entire time and giving fun directions to the others so that everyone was busy.

Mrs. Palmieri soon joined in the laughter, and moments

later Dan found Ted and himself singing "Jingle Bells" with
Rita and a hulking Babbo Natale (as Mrs. Palmieri kept
repeating), a giant Father Christmas who did not even
resemble the friend he usually called Moose. Furthermore, he
was giving no thought at all to how anyone was going to
handle anything. Santa Claus was doing that, and he was
doing it very well indeed.

Then the three young men sat on the sofa while a jovial
Santa started handing out gifts for the two Palmieris to open
—dolls and doll clothes, little dresses, a new winter coat that
miraculously fit an even more stunned Mrs. Palmieri, and so
on. Moose somehow had put such an amazingly perfect
Christmas together that little Rita was simply beside herself.
Her mother too was overwhelmed by it all, and as she started
to express her gratitude she broke into tears.

Taking hold of Moose's big hands, she gazed up into his
gentle eyes and began repeating in her soft Italian accent: *"Dio
ti benedica! Dio ti benedica, il mio largo amico!* God bless
you, my large friend!" And then, in almost the same breath;
"Ma perche? But why?"

And big Moose, looking down, wrapped his arms around
her and held her close for a moment. Then, moving carefully,
he lifted her away, looked down at her, and in a voice still
filled with laughter and happiness, though choking with some
great emotions of his own, he spoke.

"Because it's Christmas, Mrs. Palmieri. It's a time for
giving and a time for love."

"But—but—" she questioned through her tears, "who are
you? To what does a *nessuna*, a nobody such as I, owe the
honor of your visit?"

"Mrs. Palmieri, you are a great woman, and it is we who
are honored to be in your presence. Thank you for having
such a beautiful daughter, and thank you for letting us be
here."

"But—but who are you?"

The three of them grinned. Then Ted spoke. "Just Santa and a couple of his helpers, ma'am, having our best Christmas ever."

"Now we must be on our way," Moose directed, "but —"

"Moo — Santa," Dan corrected himself. "Before we depart, I for one wish to express to this fine lady and her sweet daughter my fervent hopes that they have a most memorable Christmas and a most prosperous New Year."

Mrs. Palmieri looked at Dan, smiled, shook his hand, dried her eyes for perhaps the hundredth time, and then shook Ted's hand in turn.

"I don't have Dan's gift for words," Ted said simply, "but I hope all this will help bring you a little happiness. It surely has us."

Without speaking, Moose moved forward, lifted the tiny Rita into his arms, and with his free hand reached inside his suit.

"Merry Christmas from me too," he grinned, at the same time winking at his friends. "And here's another little something that I almost forgot. Mrs. Palmieri, I have one more gift here, and I hope you and Rita . . ."

And Moose handed the speechless woman a white envelope.

"Wh — what is this?" Mrs. Palmieri finally asked with trembling voice. "I am afraid to ask, but I am afraid to open it as well. What more could such a person as I ever hope to expect?"

Intrigued, Dan glanced first at Rita and then up at Moose, who, beneath his white whiskers, had become serious.

"Mrs. Palmieri," Dan urged, "open it, please. I am as overtly curious as you. This is *one* gift concerning which Santa gave me no prior disclosures."

Sitting down on the worn-out sofa and lifting little Rita onto her lap, Mrs. Palmieri tapped the thick envelope and then carefully and with shaking hands tore one end away.

Reaching inside, she pulled out a bundle of papers, looked at them, and then, screaming, jumped to her feet and literally flew at the startled Santa.

Leaping up and throwing her arms around his neck she pulled him down, kissed him soundly, turned on a thoroughly frightened Dan and hugged and kissed him just as thoroughly, repeated the process as well with an embarrassed Ted, and then leaned against the towering Santa's chest with her arms around him while her tears flowed freely.

And it was hard to tell that she was smiling and laughing, because she was sobbing too, only it wasn't hard at all because it's always easy to see joy, and Dan and Ted knew it and saw it in her face and saw it too when they looked up at a smilingly tearful Santa Claus whom everyone else they knew called Moose Millett.

"I cannot believe it!" Mrs. Palmieri at last exclaimed through her tears. "No, I cannot believe it, but it is true! It is true! Oh, thank you! You are the answer to my prayers.

"And Babbo Natale, *Dio ti benedica, Dio ti benedica!* God bless you both! I thank each of you as well, also from the very bottom of my heart! But—but—who *are* you, and how did you know? Please tell me so that I can thank you properly."

"We're already thanked," Moose responded easily. "You're smiling the prettiest smile I ever saw, Mrs. Palmieri. That makes little Rita smile as well, and what more could good old Santa Claus and his assistants ever ask—"

"But I must know who you are! I must! No one has ever shown such love, such *preoccuparsi* . . ."

And then at last Dan got a look at the bundle of papers in Mrs. Palmieri's hand, and he was as stunned as she had been. Ted was surprised as well, even though he should have known. Somehow Moose had accomplished the impossible.

The papers Mrs. Palmieri held were travel agency schedules and two round-trip tickets—destination, Rome, Italy. Furthermore, they were made out in the names of Mrs.

Palmieri and her daughter, they were dated two weeks hence, and they were *stamped paid.*

"Moose," Dan gasped, "how on earth . . . ?"

But the giant Santa who towered above his friends had one finger over his lips signalling silence and all four fingers and one thumb of his other huge hand on Dan's shoulder, squeezing, and Dan had no choice but to become instantly silent.

Then, sensing that the time was right, Ted stepped forward and cleared his throat. "Ma'am," he said softly, "perhaps this will help as well."

He then handed the tiny woman another envelope.

Trembling, unable even to comprehend the remarkable experience she was having, Mrs. Palmieri accepted the envelope and slowly opened it, extracting five crisp new one-hundred-dollar bills.

She gasped and broke down again, and it was now Moose's turn to join Dan in being surprised. In silence the two of them gazed at the money, knowing how much there had been originally, wondering how Ted had accomplished this.

"This should help you on your trip," Ted continued quickly. "All the senior guys at school wanted to be here personally, but we thought it might get a little crowded, so I— *we*, I mean, are representing them. Merry Christmas, Mrs. Palmieri."

Finished with his much-rehearsed little speech, Ted stepped back and draped his arm around the unbelieving and finally speechless Dan's shoulder.

Weeping and thanking them in Italian, Mrs. Palmieri once more made her rounds, hugging and kissing each of the young men again.

Sensing that something special was happening, Rita bashfully hugged Dan and Ted, and then without hesitation she climbed into Moose's arms. "Santa," she said brightly as she clutched him and one of her new dolls, "I've changed my mind. You *are* nice. Are you really Babbo Natale?"

In response Moose blinked, two tears of happiness rolled down his cheeks and into his white whiskers, and for one last time he hugged Rita and Mrs. Palmieri, who somehow could not stop her own joyous weeping.

And suddenly and for no reason they could explain, neither could Dan or Ted.

Moments later, as a still weeping and thanksgiving Mrs. Palmieri closed the door behind them, the three friends cautiously made their way down the icy steps. At the closed gate they stopped, and as Moose reached for the latch, Dan spoke.

"Well, my friends, you did it. You surely did. I am overwhelmed at this most recent experience. I sincerely consider this to be one of the most outstanding moments encountered during my brief span of years, and my mind is boggled by the magnanimity of the thing. Would either of you care to tell me how it was done?"

"Well," Moose responded as he swung open the gate, "I know you'll find out soon enough anyway, so if you'll promise not to spread it around the school, I'll tell you at least about my part. It was actually quite easy. I just sold the T-Bird."

"You *what*?" Dan gasped. "But Moose, that car was your father's —"

"I know," Moose interrupted. "But I talked to Mom, and she thought Dad'd be pleased. She says he was always doing things like that too."

"Moose," Dan proclaimed forcefully, not even seeing the smile on Ted's face, "that was the only '55 T-Bird in the entire county!"

"It was the only way I had to get the money for Mrs. Palmieri's tickets," Moose concluded. "Dan, that little girl in there is the most unselfish . . . Well, she taught me more about caring and about Christmas than I've ever known. You might say that I owed her."

"But, my friend. . . ."

"Hey, Dan, did you see their faces? Wasn't that worth it?"

Dan was silent, and Moose continued. "The thing I don't understand, Ted, is where that other three hundred and fifty dollars came from. 'Fess up, man. Where did you get it?"

Ted, up to this point silent, stooped down, gathered some snow into his hands to mold a snowball, and began. "Well," he responded in an obvious imitation of Moose, "I know you'll find out soon enough, so if you'll promise not to spread it around school, I'll tell you my part of it."

Dan and Moose laughed, and Ted continued. "I slapped a little mortgage on my Camaro."

Ted's words, spoken so easily, slammed like silver bullets into the minds of both Moose and Dan. Before either of them could recover, he continued.

"Last night I was waiting for Mom there at Maxwell's, and I heard you, Moose, telling that blonde lady about what you'd done. It seemed like a pretty good idea, and I need to earn some blessings pretty badly. The trouble is that I owe too much on that car of mine to sell it and come out with a profit. So, Dad and I went down to the bank this morning, and after I'd told Mike Hess what I wanted to do and why, he refinanced me and I got a little cash. That's about it."

"Wow!" Dan breathed, taken by the new dimension he was seeing in Ted. "You guys set a fairly difficult path for me. If this is what being a senior means, then I'm not at all certain of the validity of my future expectations."

"Hey," Moose enthused as he threw his arms around the shoulders of both boys. "You'll do it, Dan. And Ted, that's great! Can you guys believe how cute Mrs. Palmieri was? She looks just like Rita. And talk about Italian excitement! I was positive the poor soul was going to have a coronary."

Dan stood shaking his head, not even listening. "It is beyond my comprehension, my friends, that each of you would purvey such treasures into airline tickets and cash for two complete strangers."

"Hey," Moose scoffed as he closed the gate behind them, "it wasn't that big of a deal, little buddy. I can always fix up another car. Besides, Rita was no stranger, and Mrs. Palmieri certainly didn't act like one. I've never been hugged and kissed so much in my life, and I'll bet neither of you have, either. I still can't believe how happy those two—"

Moose's speech was interrupted by the honking of an approaching car. Briefly the headlights illuminated them, and as the three turned to stare, a bright red '55 T-Bird pulled up beside Mr. Hancock's Cadillac.

Almost before the car had stopped, the door flew open, and Cassi, not even wearing a coat, jumped out and ran to Moose. Throwing her arms around him, she pressed her face against his big chest and wept.

"I'm sorry," she sobbed. "Oh, Myron, I'm *so* sorry! And even then you—you— Oh, Myron, why did you do it? Why?"

Dan, his mouth hanging open, stared first at his sister and then at the T-Bird and then back at his sister again. Ted, standing back, did the same. Moose, just as uncomfortable as the others, placed his arms awkwardly around Cassi's heaving shoulders.

"Hey," he said gently, "there's no need to cry. Come on, Cassi, be happy. I—"

And then Dan, his immediate shock past, broke in. "Wait just a cotton-harvesting minute," he cried. "Would one of you please have the courtesy to explain to my obviously feeble mind just exactly what is going on?"

"Oh, Dan," Cassi sobbed, "c—can't you see? Myron s—sold Daddy his car so that you and I c—could have it for a—a Christmas present! He—he did it for us, for me! Oh— I—"

And Cassi started crying again.

Moose, growing more uncomfortable by the moment, patted Cassi's back again much as he would have patted the back of a little child, and said nothing.

"Our *Christmas* present?" Dan questioned, hardly believing. "But—but Moose, that isn't fair to you, not after—"

"Oh, it's more than fair to me, Dan. Until I get another car, you'll have to taxi me around. The way I see it, you'll get Lady at least half the time, and that means I'll be nursing her along for some time to come. Besides, I can't think of two people I'd rather see have her."

"Well, this beats all," Ted said. "Moose, I'm beginning to realize that I still don't even know you. After what Cassi and I did . . ."

For a moment the soft darkness of Christmas Eve was silent, and then Cassi squealed and threw out her left arm. "Hey! I almost forgot! Mother told me about a mysterious gift under the tree, and Daddy gave me permission to open it before tomorrow. Can you believe it—the most beautiful watch I've ever seen!"

Looking into Ted's astonished eyes, and suddenly oblivious to Moose and Dan, Cassi continued. "It said, 'From a true friend.' Now, who do you suppose that could be?"

Ted and Cassi stood there then, seeing only each other, silent for different reasons, and neither of them noticed a giant Santa wink at a grinning younger brother who had his mouth open, ready to speak. Also, neither of them was aware when a giant meat-hook of a hand clamped down on an already tender shoulder, sending a silent but forceful message that a certain secret was to be kept, and that life and limb were at stake otherwise.

"Well," Moose said, feeling certain that he'd made the necessary impression on his friend, "we'd better be going, Dan. My mom's alone, and this is a bad night to be away."

"Myron." Cassi stepped away from Ted. "I—I'd like to make up to you all the rotten things I've—I've done. Is there some way. . . ?"

"Cassi, listen. You don't have anything to make up. I just wanted your Christmas to be a happy one."

"Happy?" Cassi cried, wiping at her eyes. "Good heavens, look at me! How could anyone be happier?"

Moose grinned, and Cassi continued. "I—I've not talked to Ted about this, but under the circumstances I don't think he'd mind if you and I—I mean, I owe you something, and if maybe the two of us . . ."

"My gosh!" Dan murmured to himself. "It's working! Moose's great scheme is actually working, and the watch isn't even a part of it. There's Cassi, throwing herself right into his arms, and I am a veritable witness to it. Why, it is amazing, simply astounding!"

"Cassi," Moose said gently, interrupting Dan's thoughts as well as Cassi's prattle, "I did what I did because I like you and wanted you to be happy. I've always wanted that."

"But—but—Myron—"

Moose held up his finger and pressed it gently against Cassi's lips. "Listen to me. I meant what I said. You are very beautiful, very special. Now Dan's going to take me home, so why don't you and that lucky Ted—"

Cassi's face froze. "I—I'll take you home, Myron."

"No, I'll just go with Dan."

"But I want to."

"I know, and I thank you, Cassi, from the bottom of my heart. But—well, it—it's not right. It just isn't. Besides, Ted's one of my best friends, and—well, you know how *that* is."

"Myron?"

"Yeh?"

"You're quite a guy. I hope you know that."

Moose smiled now. "Sure do, if suit, shoe, and neck size is how you're measuring."

For a moment Cassi stared up through misty eyes. Then without any real reason except that she was happy, she started laughing. Moose joined in, and soon all four were giggling like little kids.

When the laughter subsided, Cassi took Ted's arm. "Friends?" she asked Moose.

"You'll never have a better one," Moose answered.

Cassi, her tears flowing once more even though she was smiling, let Ted help her into the T-Bird. Ted then climbed into the passenger side, turned to Moose, nodded solemnly, and the two of them drove away.

In the heavy silence that followed the T-Bird's departure, Dan rubbed his arms to warm them and stared up at his white-bearded companion.

"But—but why?" he stammered at last. "Moose, she was yours. After all you had managed to accomplish, why . . ."

Without waiting for Dan to finish, Moose climbed into the passenger side of the Cadillac, pulled off his hat, wig, and beard, and laid his head back, smiling. When at last Dan was situated in the driver's seat, Moose looked over at him.

"Fun, huh?" he asked innocently.

"Moose!"

"I think Ted and Cassi are about as happy as Rita and Mrs. Palmieri were," Moose continued, still grinning.

"Moose, I asked you—"

"Still, I guess you were right all along, Dan. Cassi's one of the sweetest girls in all the world, but she's just not my type. Now one of these days, when I meet a girl who is . . ."

"*Moose!* I mean it! Why?"

Myron "Moose" Millett's smile grew even wider. "Be-cause," he replied, speaking slowly and savoring the warm and good feeling behind each of his words, "because it's Christmas, Dan—it's Christmas."